FESTIVE SHADOWS

Jennifer J. Morgan

Books by Jennifer J. Morgan

Libby Madsen Cozy Mysteries

FESTIVE SHADOWS

Libby Madsen Cozy Mysteries, Book 7

Jennifer J. Morgan

Secret Staircase Books

Festive Shadows
Published by Secret Staircase Books, an imprint of
Columbine Publishing Group, LLC
PO Box 416, Angel Fire, NM 87710

Book layout and design by Secret Staircase Books

First trade paperback edition: March, 2024
First e-book edition: March, 2024

Publisher's Cataloging-in-Publication Data

Morgan, Jennifer J.
Festive Shadows / by Jennifer J. Morgan.
p. cm.
ISBN 978-1649141736 (paperback)
ISBN 978-1649141743 (e-book)

1. Libby Madsen (Fictitious character). 2. Arizona—Fiction.
3. New Mexico—Fiction. 4. Amateur sleuths—Fiction. 5. Women
sleuths—Fiction. I. Title

Libby Madsen Cozy Mystery Series : Book 7.
Morgan, Jennifer J., Libby Madsen cozy mysteries.

BISAC : FICTION / Mystery & Detective.

813/.54

To my adorable, loving husband who has kept me laughing through a trying year (okay, maybe two). I don't know what I'd do if it weren't for you holding my hand. I'm brave because you're by my side. I love you beyond measure.

Thank you to my editors and the beta readers who take the time to point out the fatal flaws. I will never get over how many words are missed, or misused, even after I've read through it a dozen times. Thank you, Lee Ellison, Sandra Anderson, Marcia Koopmann, Susan Gross, Paula Webb, and Isobel Tamney--
I truly appreciate you!

CHAPTER ONE

Over the past several months, I'd found myself on more than one occasion reminiscing about the events of our winter ski vacation in Taos, New Mexico. Although it ended sadly, Greg and I still vowed to return someday soon—we loved that part of New Mexico and also wanted to continue nurturing our new friendship with Samantha Sweet and her family. She was fascinating—the baker, and quite the mystical one, I might add. Ever since our experience there, my intuitive abilities seem to have sharpened somehow. Mainly during massage sessions—my clients tell me more than they should; they always have. Is it possible that I *sense* more now?

That wasn't the case today, however. I'd just finished

my morning massage sessions when I ran into my mom in the Serenity Room. We normally see our clients relaxing with a nice cup of tea before or after their treatment, so it surprised me to see Mom curled up on the sofa with a cuppa. Julia Madsen looked over as I crossed the room. Her graying shoulder-length bob swished across her face as she used her index finger to pull it behind her ear.

As soon as she heard my voice, Shadow, my one-year-old black Labrador retriever, who apparently was keeping Mom company, perked up and intercepted me. Her tail wagged briskly as I leaned over to scratch behind her ears and tell her what a good girl she was.

Looking again at my mom, I smiled. "I wasn't expecting you. So good to see you!" I walked over, reaching out to give her a hug as she stood up. "Are you getting a treatment?"

"Nope, just wanted to stop by and take my girl to lunch. If that sounds good to you?"

I lifted my left arm to check my watch.

"I already checked with Bella. You have a few hours' break," she said, smiling.

I watched incredulously as she bent down to pet Shadow, wondering when she'd stop trying to organize my life. Before I could utter a word, she further informed me, "And Bella said she'd take Shadow out for a walk during her lunchtime."

I chuckled. "Wow, you've thought of everything. Sure! I'd love to have lunch. Where are we going?"

"We'll meet Jordan over at this cute new brunch place near her house."

And there it was. Mom hadn't stopped out of the goodness of her heart to take *me* to lunch. Instead, I was probably about to be ambushed by her and my sister. I'll back up a step. Jordan and I get along well enough, but she and our mother are so much alike and I'm the odd one out between the three of us. Generally that means they gang up on me, telling me how wrong I lead my life. Well, maybe that's a bit of an exaggeration. Let's just say that Jordan has always been my overbearing older sister who tends to make life a competition. When she divorced several years back, during her pregnancy with her fourth child, I thought perhaps her perfect homemaker persona might end. Nope. She, and my mother, harp on me all the time to settle down, get married, and have children. Apparently, that's the measure of success. Jordan, in particular, doesn't understand why I'd choose to run a business over being a stay-at-home mom. I have the utmost respect for those who choose, like her, to do that. But I also am realistic—that's simply not me. I wish my family would finally get that through their heads, too. My late father would have understood.

I realized by Mom's expression how long I'd zoned out after her question. "Uh, where?" I think we were still discussing where lunch would be.

"C'mon, I'll drive," she picked up her purse and led me out through the lobby.

I gave our receptionist, and my roommate, a piercing side-eye as we passed her. Bella, of all people, should have realized she needed to warn me when my mother had big plans up her sleeve. Even though Bella has only been in my life for about a year, she understands well about overbearing mothers.

Bella shrugged and mouthed *sorry*. I gave her a smile to let her know I wasn't truly angry. After all, I was hungry and I always enjoy trying new places.

* * *

Jordan and her four children were already waiting at a large table in a side room at Basil & Beets. Her youngest was three, close to turning four—Ryan was born literally the day before we opened Dharma Inspired Day Spa. Her next youngest was Chase, who had recently turned eight. And then, the eleven-year-old identical twins, Apple and Annie who were growing rapidly. I did a double-take, stunned by how much they were already maturing. Their eyes were intent on their iPhones and they still hadn't noticed me admiring their beautiful spring flowered dresses. *How is it that these two look more adult every time I see them?*

I went around the table, hugging Jordan, mussing up the boys' fine blonde hair, and giving all my nieces and nephews kisses on top of their heads as I passed them by. I sat down next to Apple at the same time both she and her sister were grumbling about handing over their phones to their mom. The twins got new ones for Christmas, which quickly became a whole new discipline strategy for their parents. Mealtime is off limits and Jordan enforces it strictly.

"You've been here before, Jordan?" I asked.

"My new favorite place," she said, holding up her blackberry basil tea. "My, uh, new *friend* brought me here right after they opened."

I caught onto her *dating code*. She had previously shared with me that when the kids were with their father, she was venturing back into the dating world. It took her a while, especially after a really creepy guy tried making friends with her while she was going through the divorce. She'd thought he was a nice man. In the end, that wasn't the case at all and now he's spending time behind bars. That cured her from wanting to date, at least until now.

We perused the menu and everyone ordered. I got half a turkey salad wrap and a cup of beet gazpacho that sounded interesting. After Jordan raved over their tea, I had to try that as well. I looked over at our mom, who brimmed over with excitement.

"What is it, Mom?" I chuckled. "You appear to have some news." I looked over at Jordan and ribbed, "Isn't she giddy?"

Julia placed both hands on the table in front of her, saying, "Well. You'll never guess what Margie and I have been up to."

Both Jordan and I encouraged her to go on. We were certainly intrigued because Julia is not typically secretive about anything in her life.

"We've been knitting! And crocheting…" she prattled on, explaining how they've been creating all kinds of fun hats, sweaters, stuffed animals, blankets, etc., for children. She reached into her purse and pulled out a blue-green funny floppy crocheted bunny rabbit with long arms and legs and wore the cutest pair of red plastic-rimmed glasses. It was adorable. She passed it around the table for the kids to see before our food arrived.

"You see, we have been donating items like these to organizations who provide children comfort while undergoing treatment at The Children's Hospital. We've actually started a charitable business now, too. It's called *Stitches of Love*." She smiled proudly, then her eyes followed the floppy rabbit as it passed through all her grandchildren's hands.

"Wow. Mom, this is fantastic. But that's not exactly

new—you've been knitting and donating to the hospital for years."

"Yes, but now we're officially a 501c charitable organization. We've just taken our crafts a step further now. I mean, we had to come up with something during the pandemic to pass time. Other than our spy games, you know." She giggled, taking a sip of tea from her glass.

I chuckled to myself, remembering about a year prior and how I was actually concerned for my mom, thinking she'd lost her mind. You see, there was a rash of break-ins in their senior neighborhood community, and they decided they'd take things into their own hands. If you could picture it, two ladies in their seventies, dressed in all black with night vision goggles—slinking around their yards, spending their time spying on the comings and goings of the neighborhood. Ultimately, they started a Neighborhood Watch, involving all the residents, and the police. At least that helped ease my mind once the police were involved. That certainly helped, but in the end, it was my black Labrador, Shadow, who sleuthed the culprits out from their hidey holes and into the confines of the law.

"I, for one, am thankful you're knitting." *Much safer than past ventures*, I thought to myself.

"So, the bigger news is that we're considering setting up a booth at the Spring Arts & Crafts Festival this year. All proceeds to be donated, of course."

Jordan's ears picked up. "Oh, I love that festival! It's *huge* … we go every year."

Our mom considered Jordan's comment for a moment. "You go to the Mesa one each year?"

"Oh, no … I forgot they have that one now."

"Yes, we're considering the one right here in Mesa.

You know, it's gotten quite large over the years, too. They have some great entertainment now … music, magic, and comedy."

"Yes! We've applied for a booth, too, for Dharma Inspired," I added.

My sister's face squinched up. "Why would a massage parlor be at an arts and crafts festival?" she questioned. She never has quite gotten on board with my profession.

"Jordan, there are many types of businesses that promote themselves there," my mom cut in before I could.

The mother of four leaned in and whispered, as though her kids couldn't hear her, "You can't give *massages* in public!"

I laughed. My sister had become so opinionated over the years. Maybe that's what becoming a parent does? I don't know, but it was strange, even for her. "Jordan, we wouldn't be giving full body massages out in public. Don't worry. We'll set up a couple of massage chairs where people can receive shoulder, neck, and arm massages. Fully clothed, I promise."

She scoffed, looking around the table at her children. No one was paying her much attention. Ryan was coloring. Chase was tearing up pieces of his napkin, probably preparing spitballs for what was going to come next if the meal didn't arrive soon. The twins were interested in the festival, though, and asked their grandma if they could help in her booth.

We continued the festival chat throughout the lunch. I shared what I knew since we'd received several communications from the Parks and Recreation department, practically begging us to consider renting a booth this year. Not remembering all the details, but sure that they had offered us substantial discounts, which made it enticing to sign up, I told her to mention that when they called.

Grandma promised Apple and Annie weekend shifts at her booth as Jordan and her kids said their goodbyes after lunch. Mom drove me back to the spa and came inside, where I copied the flier information we had. I had to get my room ready for my next client, so I left Mom talking with my partner, Alexis, about her charity work for the hospital.

CHAPTER TWO

Bella got home not long after Shadow and me. I was starting dinner when she walked in, shoulders hunched and looking exhausted. She threw her backpack down on the sofa and came into the kitchen to grab a beer out of the refrigerator.

"That bad, huh?" I asked.

When I saw the look of confusion, I added, "Oh, it's just that you don't normally drink beer on a Wednesday night. In fact, you're usually at school—bet since graduation that's a little hard to get used to."

"It has been different—not having any study group time or evening activities. But, that's not the reason for the beer. A lady from Mom's facility called me today. She wants me to come visit her." Bella's face contorted. She looked miserable.

I set down the vegetables I'd just pulled from the refrigerator onto the countertop. I took a few steps closer to her, staring her straight in the eyes. "Why?"

Using the handheld bottle opener, she popped the lid off her Four Peaks Kilt Lifter. She took a large swig, pulled a chair out, and sat down at the kitchen table.

"Honestly, I'm not sure. The lady on the phone said Mom's been much more clear-headed and responding well to her therapies."

"Are you seriously considering this?" I asked.

She nodded, looking embarrassed.

I pulled out the chair next to her and sat. "Hey, that's okay. Totally your choice to do so. I'm a bit surprised—that's all."

"I know. Me, too." She swallowed more of her drink before she continued. "But, she's my mom. It's really hard."

"I can't even imagine. The two of you have been through so much. Do you think things have really changed so quickly?"

"I'm not sure. Is a year of treatment and therapy enough time to fix a lifetime of trauma for us? I can't imagine it is."

I nodded in agreement. There wasn't much more I could add to that, but I let her talk it all out as we chopped vegetables. She weighed the options—the benefits of establishing a new relationship, or whether it was even possible. Bella had been undergoing her own therapy and, from my viewpoint, this would be an enormous setback to her progress. But it wasn't my decision. My job was to be a good friend and listen.

We continued the conversation as we both put together an entrée salad, complete with grilled salmon and some extra crispy onions on top. I poured myself a glass of white wine and we enjoyed our meal.

Once done, I asked, "Any job leads since graduation?"

"I've completed so many applications, but no callbacks yet."

"I'm not disappointed—we'd rather keep you at the spa for as long as possible." I smiled, knowing she'd rather put her EMT certification to good use instead.

"I love working at the spa, but you know I'd rather work for a hospital, fire station, or ambulance service as my full-time job. Depending on where I land, it may be possible to help at the spa too. We'll see..."

She got up, cleared the dishes from the table, and put them in the kitchen sink. Then she grabbed the cookie jar from the counter.

"Oh boy, who knows how old those are..." I said, cringing as she set it down on the table.

"No, I cleaned *those* out. I baked some fresh this morning before my shift." She gave me a huge smile as she pulled out a chocolate chip cookie.

"Oh my, those look delicious!" I grabbed a couple, trying to ignore Shadow at my feet, looking at me pleadingly. I got up and reached for her own cookie jar. "Okay, okay ... here you go." She snatched the biscuit right up and waited for another.

Bella changed the subject. "Earlier, someone from the City of Mesa called for Alexis. It was shortly before I left, and when I walked by her office, it didn't sound like the conversation was going all that well. Could that be about the booth at the festival?"

I shrugged. "No idea. Last I knew, she had submitted our paperwork. I think we were only waiting for our booth assignment. We're all paid up, I know that."

"Hmm. Well, Alexis wasn't happy when I left, that's for sure."

We finished cleaning up after dinner, and then I took Shadow for a walk around the neighborhood. We hadn't been on our usual run this morning because I had an early appointment. Poor girl, I had to leave her cooped up at work most of the day. While walking, I gave Lexi a call. It was past her six-year-old son's bedtime, so she might answer.

She did, and I learned a clerk gave her a difficult time about our festival application. They had concerns about a massage business not fitting the vendor criteria. My sister's words from earlier came crashing back.

"Anyway, I've invited Heather Knox to come to Dharma Inspired tomorrow and see for herself and meet us both in person. We can assure her that our business has every right to promote ourselves at their event."

"What time?"

"Well, I saw your last morning session ends at ten, so I've asked her to stop by around that time."

"Okay, sounds good. Anything we need to coordinate ahead of time? Messaging ... that type of thing?"

"I don't think so. I imagine she's got it in her brain that we're some sketchy massage parlor that you'd see in a bad movie. We just need to give her a tour—maybe demonstrate the type of shoulder massages we'd give to festival participants and show her the literature we'd be handing out?"

"Yeah, that sounds reasonable enough to me. I can't imagine what the issue would be."

* * *

The next day after my session was complete, and I was saying goodbye to Mrs. McAllister in the lobby, Bella and I watched two ladies approaching the building. They'd exited from a white GMC SUV with dark tinted windows. Definitely could have been a government-issued vehicle. They were giving the Dharma exterior much scrutiny, so I figured this had to be the city officials.

The more mature of the two ladies had a short silver pixie cut, thick black plastic-framed glasses, and wore heavy makeup. She was probably close to a size 18, dressed in an attractive black pantsuit with a cornflower blue flowered top under the jacket. She appeared to be the one in charge.

The younger woman at her side looked like she could still be in high school, but was probably early twenties. She was petite, slim, with shoulder length black hair showing bright red streaks throughout. She wore trendy jeans with a cute yellow top. I saw white earbuds in her ears, and she held onto a clipboard, appearing to be making some notes. She stopped, reached in her pocket, and pulled out a tin. She offered the other lady whatever she had—the one in charge waved her off impatiently as the youthful one popped something in her mouth.

In one fluid move, she returned the tin to her pocket and reached for the door, holding it open for her boss. The lady with the black-rimmed glasses approached the desk swiftly.

"I'm here to see…" her voice boomed, then stopped, and she looked over at her companion.

"Alexis Johnson. Libby Madsen," a sweet voice answered softly, reading from her clipboard.

"Hello. I'm Libby Madsen," I greeted. "And you are?"

"Heather Knox," she answered, her voice echoing

through the lobby. "This is my assistant, Bailey Young. We're here from the city for the inspection."

Bella's eyebrows rose. I gave her a slight nod letting her know I was aware of the visit.

"Very nice to meet you ladies," I addressed as professionally as I could, and then turned back to my friend. "Bella, can you please let Alexis know they're here for the tour?" She nodded and immediately picked up the phone.

I ushered the two ladies to our left and around the front counter.

"Please, this way ..." I opened the frosted glass door and led them into the Serenity Room. I stopped several feet inside the door, letting everyone's eyes adjust to the softer lighting. Both women's eyes scanned the cozy room and locked in on Alexis who'd just come through the door at the back. "And, here's Alexis now," I announced. Shadow followed right next to her.

My friend and business partner looked radiant as she crossed the room. Her glowing mocha complexion was enhanced by her warm and inviting smile. I realized she put me to shame in the style department. I always wore my typical leisure wear—yoga pants and tank top. Today was no exception. She wore a beautiful apricot silky flowered maxi-dress with varying shades of brown. As she approached, Heather seemed mesmerized watching Lexi and the flowing fabric gliding around her effortlessly. I caught the lady visibly shake herself back into the conversation.

After the introductions, which had to include Shadow or she wouldn't settle down, we walked them through the entire establishment and talked about our processes. We even took them next door to get an idea of how we help the patients from Healing Solutions, the physical therapy business that rented a portion of our building from us. Once done, we brought them back to the Serenity Room, and I poured them some tea. Shadow behaved, making herself comfortable at Bailey's feet.

As I was making the tea, I overheard Heather's questions.

"So, if I have it right—there are four massage therapists who work here. Two administrators who split shifts, and that's it. Six employees total?"

"Well, we employ four ... Libby and I are the owners."

I noticed earlier that the city employees were relaxed during the tour, but now at least one of them was getting a little feisty again. I delivered their tea and listened as Lexi answered questions about our staff. Before I took a seat, I had to ask, "Heather, do you mind if I ask a few questions?"

She gave a slight nod and gestured for me to continue.

"What exactly are you looking for in order to approve us to have a booth at the arts festival? I really don't understand this visit."

She and Bailey looked at each other briefly. Then Heather set down her teacup and pointedly looked at me. "Ma'am,"

"Libby. Please."

"Libby, there's a lot riding on this festival. We cannot take chances that any of our vendors will sour the atmosphere. It's a family event and we must ensure it stays that way."

"Okay. Sure, I understand that. We're a close family unit here at the spa, too. I know for certain none of our employees will *sour* anything. Now, are you giving scrutiny to the craft beer vendors as well? Several beer gardens are expected to be present throughout the area. What about that for souring the family mood? Maybe this is more about vendors who bring in the most money for the event, or are you truly promoting Mesa's small businesses?"

Alexis shot me a look. Shadow even cocked her head at me. I shrugged. *What?*

Bailey tapped the white plastic in her ear and said, "This is Bailey." She answered the call as she got up and started walking to a corner of the room. "Yes, we'll be right there." She turned to Heather. "Ms. Knox, we've got to go now."

Heather stood abruptly, smoothing out her pantsuit. Shadow startled and barked, but quickly came to my side when I called her. Heather ignored my question entirely and instead only addressed Lexi. "We'll be in touch, Mrs. Johnson. Good day."

They walked out through the doors into the lobby without answering Lexi's remaining question on timing. The festival was one week away.

I stood staring out the front door, skeptically. Shadow let out a growl.

CHAPTER THREE

Later that evening, after dinner, my boyfriend Greg called. It had almost been that two-week point we said we'd never go longer than—we were due for a visit. Question was: do I go to his home in Heber? Or will he come to mine in Mesa? That was always the question and all I can say for sure is that long-distance relationships are very difficult to maintain.

Immediately, I learned the answer. He explained that a colleague who worked at the USDA-Forest Service office in Mesa was going out on short-term disability. They needed someone to fill in for him; Greg put his name in the hat and got selected.

"Oh, that's exciting! Sounds like you'll get to stay around for a little longer this time?" My voice was giddy.

"They said two months minimum, but there's a possibility of it lasting up to six months."

"Oh!"

"I can get my own place, if that's a problem. I get a stipend for housing, so please don't worry about that."

My heart dropped. "No, silly, I'm not worried about that at all. And I hope you'd want to stay with Bella, Shadow, and me."

"If it's okay with you, that is what I'd prefer," his deep voice purred.

Goosebumps filled my arms. "Of course! When are you arriving?"

"Is tomorrow too soon?"

"Not at all."

We talked for another half hour. I filled him in on lunch with Mom, the festival, and he agreed he could help with the setup for both. And, depending on his schedule with the Forest Service, it's possible he may put in some volunteer hours with us as well.

Bella walked in not long after I hung up, so I filled her in on Greg staying with us for a while. She loved the idea, but also was concerned that she may have already overstayed her welcome in my home, too.

"Hey, don't worry about that. You pay rent and do your fair share around here—I think we get along great, and mostly, I want to help you out. So, please don't let that concern you. You'll know when it's the right time and I'll be here to support whatever comes. Now, did you respond to your mom's request yet? Or…?"

"Not yet. Thinking it through." The twenty-something still looked bothered. "I have my therapy session tomorrow afternoon. I think I'll talk it out there first."

"That sounds like a very smart thing to do. There's nothing that says you *ever* have to see your mother again. You know that, right?"

She nodded, but avoided answering. "I'm going to hit it early ... it's been a long day."

"Good night!" I called after her as she headed down the hallway.

I took Shadow outside and sat in the cool spring evening. Super-hot temperatures were only a couple months away now. I couldn't help but think how nice it was to enjoy a little nip in the air right now. I threw the ball for Shadow several times and then she simply dropped it by the back sliding door. That was the signal she was ready for bed, too.

* * *

We completed a nice trail run right as dawn broke the next morning. It was chilly, but so welcome as we exerted ourselves for two miles in the desert before running through neighborhood streets and back home for a hot shower and a cup of coffee.

The phone rang. It surprised me since it was still so early, but I saw Greg's name on my display.

"Wow, you're up early!" I exclaimed when I answered.

"Yeah. Excited, I guess. I'm all packed up—mind if I get there earlier than what I told you last night?"

"Come on down! I need to be at the spa by eight-thirty. If you make it here by then, great. If not, just stop in there and I'll leave an extra key with Bella at the front desk."

"Sounds good ... I'm heading that way then. See you in a couple of hours."

"Travel safe!" I said and hung up.

Looking around the living room and kitchen area, I knew I hadn't deep-cleaned in quite a while, but upon inspection, things weren't so bad. Bella must have vacuumed, or else there'd be Shadow's black hair everywhere. I went into the bedroom and pulled off the sheets and shoved them into the washing machine. After my shower, I did a quick scour of the bathroom surfaces and called it good.

About an hour later, Shadow and I loaded up in the car, pulling up at the spa exactly at eight-thirty. No one was at the front desk yet, so I wrote a note on a Post-It—'key for Greg'—and left it near the keyboard. Shadow led the way back to the office, where I dumped all my personal stuff and then we proceeded to the massage rooms so I could get everything set for my first appointment. I heard Alexis arrive and shouted out a 'good morning' to her. Shadow barreled out of the room with a low woof and I could see through the doorway that she greeted our friend with a nice slobbery kiss.

After setting her belongings down, Lexi found me washing my feet in the sink. A necessary protocol prior to giving a barefoot massage.

"Hear anything back from the Chamber?" I asked.

"Not a word. I'm thinking of heading over there between appointments. This is ridiculous—we have less than a week now to be ready for the festival and we don't have our booth assignment. They've already cashed our check, and yet *now* they're questioning our application?"

"I know; exactly what I was thinking. Anyway, I'll check in with Mom today and see how their application process is going." I finished scouring my feet and swung around to grab a towel. Hopping down from my stool, I slipped my feet into nice clean slippers. "Oh, I forgot … guess who's coming to town for several *months*?"

Her eyes drifted upward, contemplating. "I have no idea…"

"Greg! He's getting an assignment here in the valley."

"Forest work? Here?"

"They have an office here in Mesa actually … near Higley and University."

"I had no idea. Wow, that's fantastic! It will be great having him close by. Is he moving in finally?"

A tingle ran up my spine. I hadn't exactly heard it put to me that way yet, and I wasn't sure how I felt about something so formal. "Well, he's not moving all his stuff down from Heber. It's a temporary assignment. But, yes, he is staying with me," I casually said, but feeling the hesitation in my voice.

"Oooh, this is only the beginning. You watch, he's moving in!" she ribbed.

"I don't know about that. Sure, it's been more than a year now that we've been seeing each other. But isn't that way too soon? Let's not rush it."

Lexi rolled her eyes saying, "Okaaay…" She laughed and walked out. Shadow followed her diligently to the office. The spa dog knew where we kept her treats.

At the end of my session, several people immediately confronted me. Kathleen, one of our other massage therapists, wanted to know if I could cover a session for her later in the afternoon. Alexis had been to the permit office and wanted to see me right away. Bella handed me a sweet note from Greg. Shadow jumped up to give me a kiss.

The note read: Sorry I missed you. Got the keys and

have made myself at home. I'll see you after work. Love you! Greg

A tingle danced inside of me.

I affirmed with Kathleen that I could cover her massage session, and then Shadow followed me into the office and we found Alexis focused intently on her computer screen.

"Oh, hey…" she said, barely looking up. She typed a few more words and then pushed back from her keyboard and looked up at me. "You're never going to believe this, but I walked into the permit office, ready for an argument, and instead, the lady at the desk said there was no issue with our application. She confirmed our booth spot and handed me this vendor packet." She held up a large white envelope that appeared quite thick. "I questioned the reasoning for the visit from Heather and Bailey … and get this … she knew *nothing* about the visit. In fact, I don't think she even knew who they were. It was weird."

"So, are you saying that no one ever held up our application for approval?" I asked.

"She never said those words, but that's the impression I got."

"Hmmm. That is odd. Well, I'm glad we're all set then."

I remembered I still hadn't contacted my mom yet to see if they had been successful in getting their booth. I'd have to do that later. Glancing at my watch, I saw my next client was due any minute. I excused myself and ran off to prepare.

Several hours later, after back-to-back appointments, including the one I covered for Kathleen, I finally called Greg. He was cheerful and informed me he'd already picked up dinner—sushi from our favorite place close by. I was so relieved after a full day's work. After cleaning up the session rooms, checking my schedule for tomorrow, and gathering my stuff, I found Bella straightening up at the front desk.

"Going to join us for sushi?" I asked her.

"Oh, no. Greg asked me, but I had already made plans."

"Going to visit your mom?" I wondered.

"Uh, no. Just getting together with a friend of mine." The coy look that crossed her face told me it was a male *friend.* Call it intuition.

"Cool. Ready to roll? I closed everything back there; if you're ready, we can lock up."

She nodded, grabbing her purse from beneath the desk. Last year, we had experienced a couple of scary incidents, including a break-in where someone attacked Alexis. Since that time, we have had the two-person policy. Meaning, no one should be at the spa all alone. Previously, Lexi and I each worked alone late at night, frequently. Never again.

* * *

Greg and I had a leisurely sushi dinner. Shadow was thrilled to have her buddy around; she convinced Greg to play ball with her out in the yard until the sun went down. I watched the six-foot tall, muscular forest ranger run around with Shadow for several minutes, remembering exactly why I was so attracted to this man. Not only is he a stunning Chris Hemsworth look-alike, and my real-life super hero, he's also the most down-to-earth human being I've ever dated. When we first met, I found myself mesmerized by his crystal blue eyes that radiated kindness, but soon learned they held deep-seated morals. That's when I remembered that saying about eyes being the window into the soul. I'd never understood that before him.

"Are you going to be bored in an office?" I asked him once they came back inside.

"Well, of course, I prefer to be out in the field—the mountains are my happy place." His head bowed for a second before he shyly met my gaze. "But I have already been thinking of the next steps."

"Next steps?"

"Libby," he reached out and gently took my hand. "It's been nearly a year now. How much longer are we going to keep up a long-distance relationship?"

My heart pounded in my chest. *Oh no, where was he going with this?*

"I've considered that maybe I should look down here in the valley. I can't see myself living in a city neighborhood, but there are plenty of areas on the outskirts of town. Maybe I do that, and spend a little more time here, where I can see you more—you know, uh, between assignments."

I stared at him, unsure of what to say. My heart told me I'd love for him to be closer. My head was where the battle raged on. Yes, it had been a year … was that long enough to consider something like a lifelong relationship? It felt too short. On the other hand, how do we get to know one another fully unless we live closer and see each other more frequently? I couldn't help it—I was afraid of losing my independence. That'd always frightened me. The thought of becoming my mom or my sister. Of having to get someone else's permission to venture out and do something on my own. To *take care of* a grown adult. Those were aspects where I felt the weakest. But I loved him, and I certainly couldn't imagine him *not* in my life.

Apparently, my silence was deafening. He stood and

paced around, looking through the back glass sliding door, watching Shadow run around the backyard.

"Maybe it's too soon?" he finally said. "I'm sorry. We'll just see how this assignment goes. And, if it lasts too long—remember, I can find a place to rent."

I wasn't proud of myself, but I never found the right words to say. The words that would comfort him, or me. He went outside again with Shadow and I put our few dishes into the dishwasher. The rest of the night we cuddled and watched Netflix. However, I still felt tension in my shoulders that exuded from the unspoken. He deserved acknowledgement from me; I knew that. I also knew I had to be extremely careful with my words. If my past had taught me anything, I understood my first inclination tonight would have been to disagree with him. To put up that barrier and chase him away. As stupid as it sounds, that felt the safest route for me—to protect my heart. How could I consider protecting mine, while potentially crushing his? However, this relationship differed from any I've had in the past. I've done much growing up since my twenties—I'm approaching forty now, for God's sake. So, what am I still so afraid of? Images of my father flashed by. That's exactly what I was afraid of. Loving a man unconditionally and having him leave. My heart ached, thinking of how suddenly my father died, and how I had struggled every day since then. I was fifteen when he had his heart attack. Logically, I knew my relationship with Greg was completely different. Still, something I'd have to work through. Something I needed to discuss honestly with him.

I fell asleep in his arms and the subject didn't come up again—at least for a couple days.

* * *

The next day at work, Lexi had made extra copies of the festival vendor packet so Bella and I could read through all the rules and details. It was fairly straightforward, but I couldn't believe everything they had to spell out for us, things like 'vendors are expected to be cordial and respectful to customers, other vendors, and festival officials.' *Isn't that obvious?* Apparently not; rules only come about because of those who haven't previously played nicely.

Bella walked into our office.

"Do we have a schedule set yet for the festival? I could put that together if you'd like?" she asked, collectively to both Alexis and me.

Shaking my head, I looked over at Lexi. I had put nothing together.

"I've been thinking about it, but no, I haven't made a schedule yet," Lexi answered. "Thank you for volunteering, Bella." She stood up and walked over to a large wall calendar, pointing out the festival dates.

We had to complete the setup by the following Thursday evening. The festival ran for one week, Friday through the next Sunday, then teardown day on the Monday morning. Lexi sat back down at the desk, but turned her monitor around while she brought up the scheduling software. Between the massage therapist staff, which included Kathleen, Diane, Alexis, and me, we'd each take four-hour shifts for the nine days. Bella and Sydney would alternate between being at the spa or handing out fliers and engaging with festival goers. We'd already started scheduling in-spa sessions based on two therapists being available each day, so it should work out fine.

We balanced it where either Lexi or I would be at the festival, in shifts, along with one of the other therapists. Bella asked about certain shifts, so we agreed she would get first pick on the schedule since she'd been at the spa the longest. Sydney had only started with us a few months ago. Once we agreed on that, we covered the hours at both the festival and the spa, and Bella went back to her desk to finalize, print, and post it for the other employees.

Lexi asked, "Did your mom have any issues with her vendor booth assignment?"

"She said they got their packet and hadn't mentioned anything about issues. Maybe the clerk you spoke to was newer and doesn't know the process?"

"I suppose. It's just weird." She shook it off, then gave me a huge smile. "Hey! How's it going, having your man around again?"

I wasn't ready for the question. She must have seen something cross my face.

"Libby? What is it?"

I sighed loudly. "Nothing is really *wrong*. It's all me. You, better than anyone, know how I am."

"Ah, you're starting the barrier thing, aren't you?"

I laughed. She really knew me better than anyone. "It's been a *year*. Can you believe that?"

"Yes, honey. I can. Because he's a wonderful man. You two *fit*."

"Do we?"

"Why are you questioning it?"

"I don't know." Turning away, I paced around, agitated. "I honestly don't know why I get this way."

"Well, start at the beginning. What happened last night?"

I explained everything from the time he arrived. Her hand flew over her mouth, eyes wide. When she removed her hand, she whispered, "You said *nothing* ... for the rest of the night?"

I nodded; my head tilted forward, embarrassed.

"Libby," she hesitated. Then, she added gently, "You know that's not fair to Greg, right?"

"Yes, I know."

"When are you going to address your feelings, then?"

"I don't know!" Getting irritated, I plopped down in the chair again with a huff. "I was afraid last night to say anything at all, for fear that I'd blow everything. I don't know how to tell him how afraid I am to lose my independence. But also, it's not like I want the relationship to end. I'm afraid if I tell him I don't want to move any faster than it's already going, he'll get impatient and leave."

"He's a very patient man, Libby. You know he's always pragmatic and easy to talk to. Just talk to him. I don't see him as wanting to rush things if you are uncomfortable."

She had a point. I knew she was right, but it didn't make things easier.

CHAPTER FOUR

The week flew by quickly. Before I knew it, we were setting up our booth at the festival grounds in downtown Mesa. The streets north of Main St. to 1st St. and then east from Center St. to Hibbert were shut down to vehicle traffic. They dedicated the city center to the Spring Arts & Crafts Festival, with booths lining each street.

JJ and Greg both donated their time and muscle in constructing the booth and hauling massage chairs from the back of my 4Runner. Bella, Lexi, and I completed the initial trial setup of how the inside would look the next morning when customers arrived. We wanted a cozy therapeutic space with soft cushiony seating, a tea-stand, and soft spa music to set the mood. Basically, it was a remote version of our spa's Serenity Room, plus display racks with some aromatherapy candles, lotions, and oils for sale. Of course, Shadow was instrumental in that as well. The festival is a dog friendly one, and all vendors prepare for the furry friends. Shadow tested out the few dog beds we spaced near the seating arrangement and she approved of the water bowl placement outside of our stall as well.

Once we were all pleased with the setup, and made sure everything fit as we hoped, we had to store valuable items in a separate secured container behind the booth. We wouldn't want to leave items in the tents overnight since our stand only had flaps that couldn't be locked. The heavy-duty plastic side panels had ties to keep from flapping in the wind, but they were not considered secure. The city had provided a metal POD shipping container for each vendor—size dependent on how much the vendor needed to store. Ours was one of the smallest offered.

While taking a break from the setup activities, Greg, Shadow, and I walked around to visit some of the other vendors and see who our neighbors were. Hundreds of booths lined each street—I'd read somewhere that nearly three hundred vendors had signed up. Ours was located nearest to the City Plaza, close to Main St. and Center St. We anticipated good steady traffic since the local light-rail stop was nearby—Alexis and I were pleased with the placement, unsure of what we would get after the earlier scrutiny.

As we walked around, we discovered the main stage where organizers had scheduled well-known local musicians to perform each evening. During each day of the festival, the schedule showed a variety of music genres playing at several stages. From country, pop/rock, easy listening, R&B, and hip/hop—I also saw some big band music on the schedule as well.

We continued the walk—through the Kid Zone, a food truck park, and, of course, many booths selling arts and crafts. It was all very exciting. We rounded another corner and found ourselves back on our row, in time to see our friends getting ready to leave.

Lexi snapped the lock shut on the storage container. Each therapist had the code to unlock it, as we'd be on different schedules. I heard a 'yoohoo' and immediately recognized the voice. Shadow wiggled, woofed, and pulled me over to get to her grandma.

"Mom, hi!" She bent down to pet Shadow, and was already giving Lexi, Greg, JJ, and Bella hugs before I got my turn. "Where's your booth?" I asked.

"We're really close." She pointed, three booths to our right, and across the lane. Margie waved at all of us and I noticed the super cute Stitches of Love banner across the front. We waved back.

Mom was excited as she exclaimed, "Oh, there's the most adorable couple next to us—" she pointed. "Their names are John and Jessica—I think they're *hippies*," she whispered the last part. "They sell these really nice-smelling bath bombs. Zen Zone Bathtime—how cute is that? There are all kinds of aromatic bath thingies. You'll have to check them out."

As she was going on about the Zen Zone, I noticed right next door to us was Pupcakes & More, which intrigued me. No one was there at the moment; they must have arrived here super early for their setup. From the signage, it looked to be a business selling organic, homemade dog food and treats. That explained why Shadow was sniffing all around their place.

Bella scratched Shadow behind the ears as she said goodbye to everyone. JJ and Alexis also left; their son Joshua was due to be picked up at the youth theater. That was the six-year-old's latest obsession—acting. It made sense to me; my godson was such a character and I could absolutely see a profession in the creative arts for him someday.

After the rest of the group left for their vehicles in a nearby parking structure, Greg and I headed back to Stitches of Love with Mom. They, too, had set up their tables and display racks with all their creations to test how everything would fit. As we helped them load product into their secure container, I couldn't help but admire the cute tote bags for the purchased needlework. Mom, Margie, and the knitting club sure put a lot into their once part-time hobby, now full-time charitable business.

Greg latched the container and turned to the ladies. "Should we all go grab some lunch? My treat."

My mother began to answer, but then got distracted, pointing across the way, saying, "Hey, isn't that … what's her name? Trixie?"

That name got my attention and my head snapped toward the direction she pointed. Greg and Margie looked confused. Shadow barked, tugging at the leash as she appeared to understand what her grandma was saying.

I only glimpsed a slight figure, dressed in all black, and wearing a hoodie. I'm not sure how my seventy-one-year-old mother could make out any details from this far away. The person she had pointed out slipped around the corner nearest the government building complex.

Mom was still shaking her head. "What was her name?"

"Violet," I said softly, peering out over the vendor

stands in the direction she'd pointed.

The person Mom was trying to remember got arrested the summer before. Distracted and still trying hard to find her, I was sure it couldn't be true. All this went back to the events where Mom and Margie started playing neighborhood spies. It couldn't possibly be her; she was incarcerated.

Greg tried again to get our attention. "Anyone interested in stopping for lunch on the way out?"

Bless him.

* * *

Once we sat down at the outdoor patio of our favorite sandwich shop, Margie exclaimed, "Oh, that one prostitute…"

Greg nearly spit out the soda he'd just sipped. I burst out laughing at his reaction, and my mom stated, "Yes! That one, Margie!"

She had to remind Greg where we'd last run into Violet (her real name), although from the beginning of those neighborhood shenanigans, I had cheekily nicknamed her Trixie. So naturally, most of my family only remembered her as such. The twenty-something was part of a dangerous group of drug-runners. Nope, that was definitely not normal for the senior community where Mom lived, which was the whole catalyst behind setting up an official Neighborhood Watch.

"So, what makes you think that was her … the person you saw at the festival?"

"She looked our direction and I swear it was her face. You know, heavy makeup—but what seemed more familiar was that haunted expression of hers."

"Hmmm. You have a great memory, Mom. I don't remember any of that. Well, yes, I remember she was a real character ... a supreme *liar* ... who nearly got me killed. But, specific features? Well, that was some time ago."

"You're right. It couldn't be her, could it? They arrested her, right?"

I nodded. "It would be surprising if she was already out. Even turning on her cohorts wouldn't have got her that great of a plea deal."

Even though Greg had been around, he remembered little about what we talked about. That was a story already told, and one we hadn't wanted to relive. Thankfully, they dropped that subject, and we enjoyed a pleasant lunch, learning much more than we'd previously known about knitting.

After lunch, Mom and Margie headed to their respective homes, and Greg dropped me and Shadow off at the spa. He was going to swing by the Forest Service office, even though he didn't officially start his work there until Monday. I kissed him goodbye, appreciating the fact that he left behind last night's conversation.

I leaned in the driver's window before he drove off. "Don't forget we're going to the Johnson's house for dinner around six. I'll walk home after work—then we'll drive over together."

"Are you sure you want to walk?" he asked.

"Yes. We need the exercise ... it's not far."

As I walked inside, Sydney smiled. "Ready for the big event?" she asked. I noticed she had yet a different bright hair color today. Last week was hot pink, today was purple ... when we originally hired her, she had radiant electric blue.

"Ready as we'll ever be!" I chuckled, passing through

the doors and into the Serenity Room.

A customer was lounging quietly on one sofa. Shadow's training was evidently paying off; she quietly strolled through the room without bothering our guest. That had taken *months* to get right. It is inherent in her nature to run right over and kiss people. Of course, I noticed how she kept glancing over as though it took *all* her willpower to keep walking forward. I chuckled to myself.

Once we made it through the next set of doors where the office and massage rooms were, I praised her and gave her two cookies. "You're such a good girl, Shadow!"

Lexi was at her desk.

"How did Joshua do today?" I asked.

"Oh, my goodness … those little kids are the cutest. We arrived in time to see a bit of their rehearsal and my heart swelled."

"When is his performance again?"

"Mid-May … you'll definitely get a ticket," she said, looking up at me. "Oh, and don't be surprised if he bombards you two with details, and most likely, he will give an impromptu performance tonight," she said, proudly smiling.

I laughed, picturing the little thespian. "I can't wait!"

The rest of the afternoon sped by; one appointment and lots of paperwork to wrap up. Then I grabbed a few last-minute supplies I'd need to take with me in the morning, and loaded them into my backpack. I hefted it onto my shoulders, secured Shadow's leash, and we headed for the door.

"Diane!" I called out, remembering to make sure someone was available to lock up since Alexis had already left. Her head poked out from one of the massage rooms.

"Yes?"

"You're locking up, right? You and Sydney?" Standing in the doorway into the lobby, I saw Sydney nodding her head.

Diane also answered, "Yep, we've got it. See you over the weekend! Looking forward to it."

Shadow and I stepped out into the cool late afternoon. I took several deep breaths, and we started across the parking lot. Shadow pulled me out of my thoughts by barking. Her nose was pointed back the way we came—at the spa. I turned and saw the figure of a petite person disappear through the doorway.

"Who was that, Shadow? One of our customers you've befriended?" I teased, scratching her behind the ears. Then I saw the hackles appear on her back. I turned around again toward the spa, but there was nothing to see. "Okay, c'mon, girl. We need to get home."

Initially she hesitated, and let out one more low woof before she let it go, and we made our brisk walk home.

CHAPTER FIVE

Since I am normally an early riser, I was eager to start. The early meeting time didn't bother me. With the festival beginning at nine a.m., all vendors were required to be downtown, parked, and booths set up no later than eight-thirty. We scheduled our meeting time for six a.m. as we had agreed to help with Stitches of Love product setup after completing our Dharma Inspired's setup. Thankfully, Diane brought a carafe of coffee and a dozen donuts.

The moment Greg and I stepped onto our vendor's row, I sensed something was wrong. First, we passed Stitches of Love and I noticed the booth was partially collapsed. Looking across the street, two other booths were also vandalized. Shadow pulled me toward my mom's booth and she started full-alarm barking. Pulling hard, I nearly tripped over the curbing trying to keep up with her. We rounded the corner behind their stall; my heart sunk. The shipping container was wide open.

Margie and Mom walked up behind me. Luckily, Greg was right there. He grabbed Margie's elbow and steadied her just before she went down. Mom stepped into the container.

"Oh, dear! We've been robbed!" she cried out.

I followed her inside. Looking around, my heart raced. It was a mess. There was little left in the metal box. Someone had destroyed whatever scattered remains were left. I picked up a blanket that someone had slashed through.

Mom started picking everything up and sorting into piles—one for the destroyed product and another for the potential salvageable items.

I heard Lexi's voice from across the street.

"Someone tried breaking in!" she hollered. Bella was walking up the street and I saw her run toward Lexi.

"Greg, stay here with Mom; let me see what's happening over there."

Shadow and I ran over to our booth. It was still erect—and from the outside, looked unharmed. We hurried around the side where our storage was. Lexi was staring at the broken lock and a large indentation in the metal. It was obvious someone used something heavy to break the lock off. We cautiously opened the door. Nothing was missing. Thank goodness.

Bella hollered, "Guys, check this out!"

We followed her voice into the tent. When we moved the side flap to step in, we saw that the concrete floor was spray painted black. It read: "Go Away!"

Staring at the floor, then each other, Lexi shook her head. "Why?"

Bella stepped out and walked to another stand that was destroyed. Shadow and I joined her. The booth sign indicated they were selling candles. The business owners were walking around, confused about what happened. I heard them surmising the wind must have come up in the night.

"Have you checked your storage unit?" I asked them. "Some vendors have been robbed. You should check."

The woman began shaking her head, and that's when it finally registered with the partner that the weather probably wasn't responsible for their collapsed booth. They immediately hurried over to the storage, and we followed. The lock was intact, and they scrambled to unlock to look inside. All their merchandise was safe.

The man asked me whether I had the phone number handy for the organizers. "We must report this vandalism. We're also going to need help to get this structure back up. This is ridiculous."

All the information was with Lexi inside our storage, but I offered to go get it. On the way back, I saw many other business owners scratching their heads, wondering what had happened at their sites. Greg was walking toward me, shaking his head in disgust.

"Who would do this?" he questioned, looking around at the mess. "Your mother is devastated. So worried that they cannot donate to their charity now. My heart hurts for them. Was Dharma Inspired hit?"

I slowly shook my head. "Someone tried, but they didn't get in. It's unbelievable that Mom's product got stolen. I mean, if someone took our stuff, it'd be upsetting, but at least it's not taking away from sick children!"

We walked inside and saw that Bella and Lexi nearly had everything in place. The cozy fuzzy carpets fit perfectly to cover the spray-painted message. I secured Shadow's lead to a ground anchor also used to latch one side of the tent. With my hands free now, I went in search of the paperwork that had the organizer's information.

I dialed the number and waited. It went to voice mail, and I left a message. I also followed that up with an urgent text message.

"This is just great! The festival attendees are going to show up in less than two hours and look at these vendors struggling to get set up," I said out loud, and to no one in particular.

Next door to us, on our right, I saw the Pupcakes & More owners had arrived. I walked over.

"Hello. I'm Libby Madsen—we're next-door neighbors," I introduced. "Were you affected? Several…"

A heavier-set woman with dark, short cropped hair turned around. She set something down and came over. I noticed her heavy eye makeup first. Then admired the full sleeve tattoos on each arm. She wore dark jeans, complete with the dangling chain that no doubt led to a hefty pocket knife. Or could be a pocket watch. No, definitely my bets were on a knife.

She reached out her hand, "Hi Libby, nice to meet you!" Her voice was gravelly, but her tone was welcoming and sweet. "Yeah, we've helped two others who had some vandalism, and we reported it to the officials. Haven't heard about theft though. Our stuff was untouched."

I began telling her about the theft at Stitches of Love when another lady walked over. She was slightly taller, maybe five-foot-eight, and had shoulder-length brown hair and green eyes. At the end of a leash she held were two chihuahuas, looking up at me cautiously.

The first woman I'd been talking to put her arm through the other one's and said, "By the way, I'm Yvette Garcia. This is my wife, Shelly Dunning. We own Pupcakes & More—maybe you've been to our store in West Mesa?" She paused and cast her eyes left toward our booth. "We were admiring your beautiful Lab," she said with a wide smile. We all turned to see Shadow struggling to remain seated in the corner, her whine telling us all we needed to know.

Shelly held her hand out to me; her voice boomed with high energy. "Nice to meet you! You said it was Libby, right?" She looked down and introduced their two pups as Chico and Pipsqueak. "We are huge animal lovers. I volunteer at several shelters, as well as running this business together."

I knelt down and gave the two little dogs some love. I noticed they were very well-behaved and socialized.

"Yeah," I pointed back to our place. "Shadow is my Lab. We haven't been to Pupcakes, but I'm very intrigued, and I *know* Shadow will be. We own Dharma Inspired Day Spa in East Mesa. With my partner, Alexis Johnson—we co-own it. Come on over for a shoulder massage later … we'll all probably need that after being on our feet all day," I invited, noticing how Yvette wiggled her eyebrows at Shelly, before they both agreed they'd be over later.

"I'm relieved that nothing happened to your place. My mother and her friend have a booth across the way," I pointed in that direction. "They had merchandise stolen. The super sad part about that is all the proceeds were going to the cancer ward at The Children's Hospital."

"No!" Yvette gasped. "That is horrible!"

Shelly added, "What was the merchandise?"

"Handmade items—knitted and crocheted hats, blankets, stuffed animals. That kind of stuff."

Both of them gasped with their hands covering their mouths. Just then, we heard a bullhorn sound.

"Vendors! Please gather…" the organizers had finally arrived; a tall man was speaking into the bullhorn. Another man and a lady stood on either side of him with clipboards. I noticed the lady was definitely not either of those who'd visited our spa.

We moved from the booth and saw all the nearby vendors emerging into the street. Mom and Margie and the Dharma crew were already in front of the organizers. Margie reached out for my arm and I whispered again how badly I felt for their loss. Mom stood on the other side of me; I could feel her tension.

"Please, everyone … gather closely. We have a few announcements to make. Obviously, everyone is aware there's been an incident."

More business owners were walking toward the ever-growing crowd. Once everyone was closer together, the man put the bullhorn down and spoke directly to the group. He informed us he had called the police and they would deal with the crimes. In the meantime, it was most important to get the fallen structures back up and have those vendors ready for business. There was one hour before the gates to the festival would open and he encouraged everyone to band together to assist their neighbors.

Everyone immediately nodded their heads in agreement, fully supporting those who had been victimized. Shelly's loud voice suddenly sounded next to me, making me jump.

She hollered out, "How many people had merchandise stolen?"

Only my mom and Margie raised their hands.

Shelly's voice resounded through the audience. "Fellow vendors—this is a travesty! Do you realize that these two lovely ladies were selling *homemade* needlework to support cancer patients—*children*! All their proceeds from this event's earnings were going directly to charity."

There was a hush that settled over the crowd as that information sunk in. I caught Greg's side-eye glance at me.

Shelly shouted again, "We must stop these monsters who did this!"

Several vendors began getting riled up and cheered Shelly on before the tall man took control again using his bullhorn. "Ladies and gentlemen—we understand the gravity of the situation and we'll do everything in our power to see that the police bring the perpetrators to justice. In the meantime, please help your neighbors, however necessary, to get their businesses up and running within the hour." He bent over slightly to hear what the lady with him had to say. Then, he finished his speech with, "Let's put this behind us for now and have a great festival—we wish everyone luck with their sales!" People disbanded, and all the vendors paired up to help those in need.

Greg leaned over and whispered in my ear, "Jeez, a little intense, isn't she?"

I nodded slightly, knowing he was talking about Shelly. "They're our neighbors—Pupcakes & More," I whispered back.

Mom turned to Shelly. "Thank you for what you said.

How did you know?"

Shelly and Yvette introduced themselves and then pointed at me. "Your daughter told us what happened. We're sick about it."

"Oh, so am I. We had such high hopes!" she exclaimed. "But we'll do the best we can with what we have. I can't imagine we'll have much to donate, though. And, I don't even know how to break this news to the directors at the hospital," her voice cracked.

Our hearts ached for them.

CHAPTER SIX

Despite the early morning drama, the first day of the Spring Arts and Crafts Festival was hugely successful and attendees were completely unaware of the earlier disruption. Music thumped from the various stages throughout. An enormous variety of ethnic food aromas wafted our direction all day, making me so hungry. There had to have been thousands of people who ventured through, and I was pleased to see how many stopped at our booth.

Bella, Shadow, and I worked the first four-hour shift in the morning. At lunchtime, Lexi and Sydney took over, followed by Kathleen and Diane, for the late shift. For the majority of vendors, the day ended around five in the evening, but the musicians kept entertaining and the food booth vendors kept feeding people until closing at ten p.m.

When I walked out of our booth at the end of my shift, the first order of business was to find those food booths and investigate the selections. Greg had arrived a few minutes prior, after having gone to run some errands while I was working.

"Ready for lunch?" I asked him, but Shadow also seemed to understand what I was saying. She wagged excitedly. "I'm not sure you can have what they serve here. But, let's go see."

Apparently, Yvette, who'd just appeared from the back flap of Pupcakes & More, overhead me talking to Shadow and Greg.

"Oh, who's the cute girl, here," she said sweetly, bending down and rubbing Shadow behind her ears. "Who wants a treat?" She looked up at me. "Mom, can Shadow have a treat?"

I laughed. "Sure, she'd love one!"

She disappeared behind the wall again.

Greg asked me, "What are you hungry for?"

"I'm not sure, but my nose tells me there are a ton of choices. Have you walked around to see yet?"

He shook his head. "Nah. Just drove up and walked straight here without really exploring."

Yvette came out with a little baggie she held up. "I couldn't decide. So, I'm giving you a sample of several of our bestsellers."

"Oh, my goodness. That's so sweet—thank you!" I said, taking the offered treats. I opened the bag, made Shadow sit, then gave her one of the cookies.

"We've had a ton of traffic today. How about you guys?" she asked.

"Not bad. I probably gave at least twenty short shoulder massages ... better than I'd thought the turnout would be. I mean, you never know, since we aren't a 'craft' business or anything."

"Yeah, no doubt. That's pretty good. Well, I'm heading out, back to the distribution center because we're nearly sold out!"

"Whoa, that's amazing. Congratulations!" Then, I remembered that I still hadn't introduced Greg, so I did that and he thanked her for their support of Julia earlier.

"Oh, of course. We're huge activists—mainly animal wellness and rights. But, philanthropy all around and we love what Stitches of Love is doing for the children and their families. We'd love to help—we're discussing how best to do that." She checked her watch. "Yikes. Hey, Shelly's really busy ... so I better hurry and get back with more product."

"Well, thank you for the treats," I held up the bag, hollering after her as she ran off. Shadow started jumping for the treats. I took out one more and offered it to her after she sat, then I turned to Greg. "I'm starving! Lead the way..."

After indulging in street tacos from one of the food trucks, we walked around, familiarizing ourselves more with all the beautiful arts and crafts. There were some amazing artists—everything from canvas paintings to blown-glass work, painted figurines, Christmas ornaments, and so much more. When we rounded the corner back to our concession row, we stopped to say hi to Margie and my mom. They had about a dozen crocheted animals displayed and a few blankets. Far less product than what was in the container last night. The two ladies were chatting with customers, so we gave a little wave and continued on.

Then I saw them. We walked up to the couple that Mom had called *hippies*—the ones who owned Zen Zone Bathtime. I first noticed him—the super thin and tall man, mostly bald on top, but with wispy, long gray strands that hung down his back. That, and a full gray mustache and beard. Behind the wire-rimmed glasses were friendly sky-blue eyes smiling at us. The lady looked like his twin, with white shoulder-length bobbed hair and similar wire-rimmed glasses. She was helping a customer as we walked up.

"I think I saw you early this morning helping those poor ladies," he said, looking to his right at the empty vendor space.

Greg answered, holding his hand out to shake. "Yes, that's right. It was a very hectic morning, wasn't it? Oh, by the way, I'm Greg and this is Libby—she has a booth over there," he said, pointing across the street. "And this is Shadow," he said, looking down.

John first greeted Shadow by holding his hand out for her to sniff. Then he kneeled down and talked sweetly to her at her level. Once he stood again, I held out my hand to shake his, adding, "Libby, with Dharma Inspired Day Spa."

"Cool, cool. My name is John. And my wife over there—that's Jessica. So nice to hang with you all this week, man."

"Curious … did you have any damages overnight?" I asked John.

"No. Nothing here. But, man … I really feel for Julia and Margie. We met them yesterday setting up—really friendly folks."

"Yeah, Julia's my mother."

"Oh! Awesome. You're the daughter she speaks of, then. Of course, she mentioned a massage business—Dharma ... got it!" he smacked his palm to his forehead. "Hey, look ... we'd love to help however we can. Dude, are you going to set up a Go Fund Me or something?"

Greg and I looked at one another. I'd been so busy all morning, I hadn't given it much thought and we hadn't talked to Mom yet. I just shrugged, but Greg shared with both of us what Margie had suggested.

"Once they've sold out the few items that remain, Margie mentioned their knitting group was already working hard to salvage some items. She indicated there may be a small stockpile that could still be sold. We'll see. Julia didn't seem to think that was possible ... or that there was enough to make a difference."

"Yeah, that's really tough. They must have already put in *hours*. That's rough, man. Well, just let us know how we can help. Our voices might not be as audible as that one over there." He pointed to the Pupcakes stall where Shelly's voice could be heard clearly. "But we love us a good charitable cause and we're here to help."

I chuckled, thinking about Shelly shouting in support during the early morning hours. She was passionate, that was for sure. "Thank you, John ... we sure appreciate it."

"Oh, here ... the missus is free. Let me introduce you to my better half," he coaxed us over closer and we stood chatting until the next customers walked up. John and Greg got started talking about wildlife—a passion for both of them. Jessica went back to selling bath bombs to customers, and my attention wandered over the passing crowd. I excused myself when I saw someone familiar.

Shadow and I quickly caught up with a lanky young

woman with red streaks in her black hair. When she stopped at a custom candle-making booth, I tapped her on the shoulder.

"Hi! Bailey, isn't it?" I greeted, and as she turned around, I saw I was right; it was definitely the assistant who visited our spa. Shadow let out a low woof.

She glared at my pup, then look up at me and hissed, "Excuse me?" she said, perturbed at the interruption. Definitely not the sweet, helpful assistant attitude today, I could see. "Do I know you?"

"Oh, right. Guess I should have started with that. I'm Libby Madsen from Dharma Inspired Day Spa."

There was a slight shrug of her shoulder, no obvious recognition, and an impatient attitude that said, ...*and?* She was clearly not interested in talking to me.

"You came by our business last week—with Heather..." I added.

She just shook her head, dismissed me by turning away and walked into the booth to look at candles.

Shadow woofed again, trying to keep her attention. It didn't work. We both stood there staring at the back of her long, jet-black hair, stunned at her rudeness. I couldn't believe she hadn't connected me with the business name— that was strange. Well, I guess we wouldn't be offering her a free massage for stopping by our booth. As we headed back to find Greg, I simply put her out of my head, rationalizing that she probably separated business and pleasure on her weekends. She hadn't wanted to be recognized; she was at a festival and who wants to talk business when there's cotton candy around the next corner?

Greg and I made our way back to the parking lot and decided it was time to relax at home. It had been a very early morning. No sooner had we walked in the front door than my phone buzzed in my jeans pockets. I pulled it out; it was Mom.

CHAPTER SEVEN

Julia Madsen has always been a determined woman. When she put her mind to something, it got done. Today was no different; she would not wallow in her sorrows over the theft. No. Instead, after selling out of the product they had at the festival, she gathered the knitting group together and collected all the goods that each lady had in stock at home. They'd gathered enough items to keep their booth open for at least a second day. From there, they'd take it day by day.

It was late afternoon, and I was exhausted, but I agreed to pick Mom up and to take her to The Children's Hospital. She wanted to talk to the director in person to explain what had happened, and she didn't want to show up empty-handed. She brought along a small box with a few miniature stuffed animals for the kids.

"I sure wish I was bringing them a big fat check instead," she solemnly said on the ride over. "Next time."

"I'm sure they'll understand. This was completely out of your control." I wondered then what the police would find. Needle in a haystack, I guessed.

Once we walked into the hospital, my mother was on a mission. I had to hop-to in order to keep up with her. Down several hallways, up the elevator to the second floor, a few more turns, and she halted, staring down the long corridor.

"Oh! Kathy Dewey with Just Ducky is here! You *have* to meet her!!!" she gushed.

Just Ducky? I wondered.

Walking toward us, weighted down with an enormous box, I saw a lady radiating delight. She had long black hair with silver streaks throughout. She was average height and, from the load she carried effortlessly, was quite athletic as well. Her aura instantly made me smile.

"Julia!" she exclaimed. "I haven't seen you in sooo long!" She quickly made her way toward us. Seeing a chair outside one of the many offices that lined the hall, she set her package on it. Then she turned and gave my mother a long hug.

She pushed back, still clinging to my mom's shoulders. "How have you been, Julia? What has it been—at least a year, right?" She glanced my way, smiling before she turned back to my mother. "I've heard about the great work you've been doing here. My goodness."

Mom blushed. "Well, we're trying … that's for sure. I'm surprised to see you in town, though. Heard Tahoe had record amounts of snow, but I guess you dug your way out?"

She laughed, then added, "It was quite the winter, yes. Thankfully, it's melted now, and I was able to get our latest donations here for the hospital's big event. I was concerned there for a while—ah, but it worked out fine." She glanced my direction again. "Julia, this must be one of your daughters? The resemblance…"

Mom quickly put her arm around me. "I'm so sorry—yes! This is Libby!"

I reached out and shook Kathy's hand. "So nice to meet you."

"Oh, I've heard so much about you and…"

Mom added, "Jordan."

"Yes, yes … Jordan. Your mom speaks the world of you two!" she said to me. "I'm so happy to finally meet you. Are you guys in the knitting club as well?"

I quickly shook my head. "No. I don't knit … guess I should learn, though, huh?" I chuckled.

Mom explained that Kathy, and her husband, Phil, started a charitable organization called Just Ducky after their ten-year-old son, Nicholas, passed away from cancer. Nicholas was only eight years old when they first learned he was sick. As imagined, she explained how grueling those two years were as they worked with many specialists, trying to save his life. During that time navigating their new normal, Nicholas and his parents saw a genuine need for all the children and their families in the hospital.

The children needed comfort and distraction. They were frightened; the procedures they underwent were scary, and then they felt horrible, too. The children weren't the only ones who were terrified, though. Every parent who sat by their child's side put on the face of bravery, while also sick with worry about their loved one. And life doesn't stop when a child gets sick; many parents have to continue their work. Bills stack up and vacation time becomes depleted. And, with all that, they also have to eat and rest their heads somewhere at night. Often, as experienced with Kathy and Phil, the procedures are performed at hospitals away from the family's hometown. So, finding a hotel and eating out all the time become a way of life. As with many families, there are other children at home to consider as well. All of it has to be handled, and that's where support systems are crucial.

Just Ducky donates thousands of dollars in gift cards and toys to children fighting cancer. The Nurses and Child Life Specialists give the donations to children having a rough day in the hospital. These donations bring a smile to a child's face and, of course, to the parents, siblings, and even the nurses and doctors caring for the young patient. It also gives these young fighters and their families the feeling that someone who has been there understands and cares about them.

As Mom relayed this, I kept looking at the lady she was talking about. My face was probably showing a look of horror. Kathy's was not. In fact, she had a glow about her.

"How did you cope through all that?" I asked her incredulously.

"Well, first … that was many years ago—nineteen years to be precise. So, time is definitely a factor for healing. It hasn't always been easy, trust me. However, as Julia explained, the work that we do to help families was not all my idea—it was all Nicholas's. He hated to see others in pain, even when he himself was going through the same struggle. What brings me joy is carrying out his wishes. I see *his* smile through every child I help. That's what gives me strength."

"Wow, I'm impressed. Thank you for everything you do for the children. Oh, and their families, too!"

Kathy turned to my mom and asked what she was doing at the hospital today. Mom gave the update from the festival and that was the first time I saw Kathy's expression change. She was visibly upset hearing what happened at the Stitches of Love booth.

"What can I do to help, Julia?" she asked with concern.

"Oh, I'm not sure." Mom glanced down the long hallway, grimacing. "I've still got to deliver the news."

"Hey, I've gotta get this load delivered as well. Please call me later, Julia … I'm willing to help however I can. I have a flight out tomorrow—but you know there's lots I can handle from home." She pulled Mom into a giant hug, then reached out and gave me one as well. "You two ladies take care. I really hope you find who stole from you—from the children! Ugh." She shook her head, then turned to pick up her box, and she was gone.

* * *

After we finished our business at the hospital, I dropped Mom off at her house and planned to stop back at our booth to see how they were faring—it was nearing closing time. First, I texted Greg.

Where are you and Shadow? I'm going to stop by the festival to check on the booth—then how about dinner? Mexican food tonight?

Kathleen and Diane were chatting up customers as I approached. I squeezed past several ladies and made my way to the side flap. When I walked in, it was immediately obvious that our products were running low. I grabbed a pad of paper and began jotting notes. The Ayurvedic oils were popular—we needed several more cases of those. I just hoped we had the stock back at the spa. There probably was not time to order more and have them delivered before the festival was over. Next, we'd need a few more candles, and if we had more incense at the spa, I'd send that along with Lexi, who had the morning shift tomorrow.

Diane turned to me. "It's been busy! Never expected so much traffic." She began straightening up; the booth would close in thirty minutes.

"Yes, we're moving through product pretty well," I said, pointing to my list. "Not much to store away tonight, I see. We'll bring more tomorrow. What about massage appointments? Are we booking anything?"

"We've handed out a bunch of cards—but I haven't had a single moment to check my phone to view the activity on the app yet."

My phone chimed.

We are at home. Mexican sounds great! What time?

I quickly tapped out my answer and said goodbye to Kathleen and Diane. As I moved the flap aside to walk through, Shelly was standing there.

"Hey, how were sales today?" I asked.

She had a horrified expression as she looked up from her phone.

"Everything okay, Shelly?"

She shook her head slowly. "They have shut our factory down, pending inspection and investigation."

"Oh, no! Why? What happened?"

"There have been several complaints about dogs being sick after eating treats they received here," she paused, pointing at the Pupcakes & More stand, "today!"

"How could that be? That's awfully fast. How would they know for sure it was from *your treats*?"

Her face paled. She just shook her head slowly, absorbing the news.

CHAPTER EIGHT

As soon as I walked into the house, I immediately sought out Shadow. She and Greg were out in the backyard playing fetch.

"How has she been all afternoon?" I asked him.

"So energetic ... I swear I've thrown this ball a thousand times." He pointed at her, running back to us with a slimy yellow-green ball. "Why?"

She ran up to me, sat, and dropped her ball at my feet. I picked up the now slobbery mess and threw it across the yard.

"Pupcakes is being shut down. Shelly said there were complaints of ill dogs who had been at the festival this morning."

"No!" Greg exclaimed. He looked toward Shadow.

"She ate a bunch of their treats."

"I know. That's why I'm concerned."

We threw the ball several more times and saw no sign of discomfort from this Lab. We went back inside so I could get her dinner together. The second I set it down, she wolfed it right up. Nothing different there—she gobbled it up as usual.

Greg put his shoes on, asking me, "Still want to go out for dinner?"

I hesitated, looking at the plastic baggie sitting on the counter, the one Yvette gave us with a sampling of Pupcakes treats. "Yeah, let me get Shadow a treat and then we'll go." I decided to grab Shadow's cookies from her own cookie jar instead, just to be on the safe side. With a 'stay' command and a cookie in her belly, she settled down into her comfy dog bed and watched us walk out the garage door.

* * *

Gringos Locos in Apache Junction was a longer drive for us, but well worth it. For a Thursday night, we found it quite busy, so we chose an outside patio seat and ordered a couple margaritas.

"How do they know the Pupcakes treats caused the dog's illnesses?" Greg asked, clearly still concerned.

"I have no idea. But I exchanged phone numbers with Yvette and Shelly and I hope they'll keep us informed. Shelly seemed legitimately concerned about Shadow. Although, she was adamant that they follow strict protocols in their factory and she felt confident there was no contamination. We'll see what the inspection uncovers."

"And, how did it go with your mom?" he asked, popping a chip into his mouth.

I filled him in on that visit—mostly telling him all about the Just Ducky organization and its founder. We both decided that was a charitable cause worth contributing to annually, it was so impressive.

"Hey, I ran into Sage today … out at the festival before I met up with you," he mentioned.

Sage Logan was a longtime friend and client of mine. Of course, she'd be at the festival; she was an extremely talented artist and longtime resident of the state.

"Does she have her work set up in a booth?" I asked.

"Nah, Shadow and I ran into her walking around."

"Oh darn, wish I'd seen her."

"Well, anyway, we got talking, and I mentioned I might be looking for some land out there at some point…"

"So, you're serious about that, then?"

He hesitated, apparently sensing my apprehension. "Yeah. It's been on my mind."

I raised my eyebrows while dipping my next chip into the fresh salsa. "You want to *move* to the valley? From Heber?"

He nodded slowly. "I think so. Eventually. Maybe keep both properties?" He took a large gulp of margarita before he continued. "Anyway, she mentioned that the five acres next door to her recently went on the market. I looked it up online and made an appointment to discuss more with the listed realtor."

I nearly spit out my sip of margarita with that revelation. I coughed, cleared my throat, then choked out, "Really?"

His expression changed from nervousness to exasperation. "What, Libby? Why do you find it so surprising that I would want to move to be closer to you?"

Oh. Dear. I've offended him.

Thankfully, the server came with our food. It was a great distraction while I gathered all the thoughts bouncing around untethered in my brain.

"Is there anything else I could get for you?" the young woman asked us.

We both shook our heads, but remained silent.

"Hon, I meant nothing by that…" I tried to lighten the mood. "It's just that … well, you've surprised me with that news, honestly. You've never mentioned *moving* here."

He stewed a little, cutting his enchilada into bite-size pieces, allowing the hot melty cheese to cool. Then he set his knife and fork down and looked me straight in the eyes.

"Do you see us as having a future together?" he asked boldly.

When I couldn't look him in the eyes, he picked up his utensils again and quietly ate his meal. I poked at mine a little, but lost all appetite. I hadn't meant to ruin our dinner out, but was at a loss for words. The rest of our evening was subdued and polite, but no furtherance of that conversation.

* * *

The next morning when I woke up, he was already gone.

Bella was on the back patio, enjoying her coffee. Shadow bounded around the backyard and nearly bowled me over when she saw me come out the door.

"Did you see Greg this morning?" I asked.

"He was in a hurry … just caught the door shutting when I came into the kitchen," she said, before noticing the pained look on my face. "Why? What happened? Are you two fighting?"

Hmmm. Fighting? I thought back to the events of last night. Voices were never raised. In fact, we just went silent. *Was that actually fighting?*

"I don't know. A disagreement, I suppose," I muttered, taking the seat next to her.

"Oh no! What about?" she asked, then turned and slapped her hand to her mouth. "No. Libby, I'm sorry! None of my business. What am I thinking?"

"It's okay," I assured. I took a sip of my coffee, sat back, and added, "I'm not sure what I want for my future. I guess that's what the problem is." An audible sigh escaped as I set my mug on a small table next to me.

"He's getting serious, isn't he?" she asked.

"Well, I wouldn't say to the point of, like engagement, or anything …" I wasn't entirely sure about that either. Then, I turned to face her. "He wants to move here. As in, buy land and build a house."

"Oh. Well, that doesn't sound so bad," she blurted out. Then retracted and said, "Or, maybe it is too soon."

I stood up and walked over to where Shadow dropped her ball. I picked it up and threw it far to the other end of the grass. She bolted and had it back to my feet in a flash.

"He's free to do whatever he wants to, of course. It's just that I know how much he loves Heber … the forest, and that community. It really feels as though he'd only be making a move here for *me*. I don't know how I feel about that. It's a lot of pressure. I mean, I've never had a relationship last more than six months—so I'm in uncharted territory as it is. How do I know this thing we have is really going to work out for the long run?"

"You don't, Libby. No one ever does. But is that a reason to *not* move forward? To see how it goes?"

"I know. And that's what we're doing—with him staying here for a month or so, right? To test the waters. Then, suddenly, he springs these other plans on me. I mean, he's already scheduled an appointment with a realtor!"

Bella nodded, sighed, and sat back, enjoying her coffee. I kept throwing the ball for Shadow. Then my phone chimed.

Libby, can you help us? Call me.

It was Yvette. I excused myself and thanked Bella for letting me vent, then I went inside the house and called the Pupcakes owner back.

* * *

I had already shut the door, and was leaning in to unhook Shadow, before I realized someone was standing at the back of my 4Runner.

"Oh jeez, Shelly … you scared the sh—" I took a deep breath. "You scared me." I looked around for Yvette, but didn't see her. Shadow wiggled, stretching to get to Shelly. She seemed to know already who the dog biscuit lady was—maybe she had a permanent cookie smell on her I couldn't detect.

"Sorry, Libby. I saw you pull in and thought we could walk together." She knelt down and gave Shadow some love. "Sorry, I can't give you any yummy treats," she cooed to Shadow in a soft voice.

I'm glad I had run into her; I was hoping to get all the details. Yvette hadn't explained other than only begging for my help.

"I don't understand what type of help I could provide. Your wife wasn't very specific—can you tell me what's going on?"

I pressed the lock button on my fob, and we started toward the parking garage exit.

"To start, you can help explain to the inspector that Shadow has had *many* of our treats—the same batches— as those who have filed complaints. If the treats were contaminated, why haven't they affected her?"

I shrugged. "Listen, I have no problem sharing our story, our experience with your products. However, there's no way for me to speak about another dog's injuries. I hope you know that, right?"

"Sure. Sure. If we can have the inspector *see* that Shadow is perfectly fine … maybe they'll reconsider the immediate shutdown." She glanced around, then continued, "Libby— our products did *not* poison any animal. I can assure you of that!"

"How can you be one hundred percent certain?" I asked.

"You need to see our facilities—know our process. Once you've been through the entire quality control area, you will know. There simply isn't any ingredient in the process that *could* harm an animal. That's the whole point! That's what our company is founded on!" Her hands gesticulated and her voice progressively got louder. Shadow and I gave her a wide berth. "I'm telling you, someone is out to sabotage us."

"Why?"

She shrugged.

"Well, who are your closest competitors? Who has the greatest motive?"

She rattled off a couple companies quickly, but never slowed down to actually consider the questions. Yvette must have heard Shelly's booming voice as we approached their place because her head peeped through the flap and she held her index finger over her lips.

"Shhhhh…" she mimicked, tilting her head to indicate inside. "We have a visitor," she indicated politely as she opened the front of the booth wider and welcomed us inside. "Shelly. Libby. This is Mr. Littel from the Office of the FDA."

Shadowed barked as soon as she saw the man.

"Bart. Just call me Bart."

The nasally high octave of his voice made me chuckle; thankfully I did so with my inner voice this time. He was a short, plump, bald-headed man, probably in his sixties, and I would have pegged him as an old-school engineer. Everything from the blue button-down, long-sleeved shirt, with dress slacks that were awkwardly placed high over his rounded belly, causing the legs to be high-waters; it all screamed computer geek. Then, to complete the look, he also wore red plastic-rimmed glasses that sat crookedly on his bulbous nose. He was honestly cute as a button. I couldn't help but think that for an inspector, he wasn't threatening at all. This shouldn't be difficult.

I got the feeling that Shelly had sized him up similar to how I had. She reached out and introduced herself as an owner of Pupcakes & More. She then introduced me and Shadow. As they began answering his questions, I felt awkward and out of place. What was my role here, actually? I got the idea Mr. Littel—Bart—was thinking along those same lines, with the way he kept glancing my direction, and then looking down at Shadow as though she may attack at any second. He didn't seem like much of an animal lover to me.

"We take complaints such as these seriously …" he was saying when I tuned into the words again. "Now, I'll need samples of the exact batches you sold from this location."

Yvette was already prepared and placed several bags of treats into a tote. Shadow's eyes followed intently, watching each being placed on the countertop.

Shelly began her defensive story. "Shadow here—she had these same treats all day yesterday. And look, she's fine." For a moment, I thought she was pulling out a treat to give Shadow. I wasn't sure how I felt about that—what if someone had tampered with the treats? I breathed a sigh of relief when she only held up the package.

Shadow heard her name, eyed the package being dangled around, which got her squealing with excitement. I'm sure she thought she was about to score. Bart scooted back a few steps, and apparently now understood why we were hanging around.

Shelly's theory did not faze him at all. "Doesn't mean your product didn't affect another dog negatively," he said matter-of-factly. He flipped a few papers over on his clipboard, then looked up and over his brilliant red glasses. "I see here your factory is in Buckeye. At…" and he looked down again as he read off the address. His bushy brown eyebrows lifted. "Is that right?"

Both Yvette and Shelly nodded.

"Inspectors will move into the facility within the next twenty-four hours. You have already been instructed to shut the facility down—no employees, including yourselves, are to be on premises without the presence of an FDA inspector escort. Is that understood?"

They both nodded again. Yvette solemnly said, "We've informed everyone."

"Questions for me?" he asked. To that, they both shook their heads. "Then, I'll need both of your John Hancocks right here." He pointed to the bottom of the last page.

Once Bart left the site, Yvette peeked out to make sure he was actually gone.

She whipped around, looking at both of us. "This is *crazy*, isn't it?" She walked to the back of the booth, held up a bag of treats. "This is no joke. They're seriously going to shut us down. Our livelihood—everything we've worked so hard for years to build!"

Shelly's head tilted forward. "All our employees. And their families..." her voice cracked; her head hung there for a second before her spunk returned. Her eyes met ours with fire. "We can't stand for this! You know they're not looking into the possibility that someone tried to set us up—they're only looking to shut us down. No other option."

"Well ... Shelly ... they *have* to look into this. You can't blame the FDA for that." I stopped abruptly when I saw her glaring at me. Realizing I didn't really know these women all that well, and even if they didn't believe their product was bad, none of us know that for sure. I tried a softer approach. "Hold on. I know ... I know. You know your product better than anyone—both of you. However, is it even remotely possible that someone tried to sabotage you? Perhaps a former employee? A competitor? Someone you've had a falling out with? Let's put our heads together and try that angle."

Yvette came closer. "Shel, she's right. While the FDA is testing the batches, we can work on figuring out the *how* and possibly the *who*. Right now, we don't know if the product is contaminated. They have accused us of that, but there's no proof yet." Her eyes moved rapidly between both of ours, waiting for an objection. "So, let's just calm down and come up with a plan that gets us farther down the road in the case they come back with proof of contamination. Either someone is making false allegations, or we have someone sabotaging our product. We need to put our heads together and figure that out."

Shadow barked in agreement. I nodded my head, and wished them good luck, before heading out.

"Wait, wait … no, we meant all three of us should put our heads together!" Shelly exclaimed, when she realized I was bowing out.

"Uh," I honestly was speechless. "What exactly do you think I can do to help? I mean, I'm more than willing to offer ideas…"

"Libby, Greg was sitting right there yesterday telling us all the people you and Shadow have helped. That's why we called you first … he said, and I quote, 'if anyone can figure out who the bad guys are, it's those two…' and he pointed directly to you."

"That's right!" Yvette remembered the conversation. "And your mother was over here earlier, telling us stories. We know you're legendary for solving crime."

"But…"

Shelly cut me off. "But nothing. Please, Libby," she pleaded.

Shadow even pouted, using her big brown eyes.

"Guys, I am not an investigator. I thank you for the praise, but honestly, I'm going to kill Greg and Julia both. Yes, there have been a few times I've been in the right place at the right time and may have put a few clues together. This is different. You need an experienced person to actually *investigate* a serious allegation."

Just then, we all heard some shouting. We made our way outside and saw the man with the bullhorn. Even with festival-goers still around, he was gathering vendors.

"At least one representative from each booth, please gather at the vendor staging area in City Hall," he shouted as he walked down our row.

I looked over and saw that Lexi and Kathleen had their hands full at our booth. I caught their attention, letting them know I was present and would attend this impromptu meeting. Walking over with Yvette and Shelly, Shadow got more excitable with the frenzy of people around. We didn't have far to go, as our booth was relatively close to the government building complex.

"What do you think this is about?" I asked.

Both the ladies shrugged their shoulders. We had caught up with the organizers and as we approached the crowd of vendors entering the city building, I saw my mom and Margie. I thought they'd run out of product and had already gone home for the day.

"How…" I started.

Mom didn't wait for the question. "Margie picked me up. Do you know what this is about?"

I shook my head just as the main organizer hushed the crowd inside the large conference area.

"Thank you! Thank you. If I can get everyone's attention…" he started, then signaled to someone in the back to close the doors. "Vendors. Thank you. If I can have everyone's attention, please."

It took several minutes for a hush to settle over the room.

"There have been many of you with concerns after last night's incident," he began. "We're here to address those concerns. Unfortunately, there are many rumors spreading and we'd like to get ahead of the fake news."

I looked wide-eyed at the Pupcakes ladies and my mom, and whispered, "What happened last night?" None of them knew.

A City of Mesa police officer took to the microphone that was handed to her from the organizer.

"Ladies and gentlemen, last night at approximately eleven-thirty, our department was called with reports of gunfire here on the festival grounds. We dispatched all units and the SWAT team. They were on scene in less than five minutes.

"Upon arrival, we cleared the area, which included all music stages and the food court. During this evacuation, chaos ensued and several festival attendees were injured. The extent of the injuries overall were minor; several people were treated onsite and released. Most of those were because of the inhalation of pepper spray. After an extensive investigation, we found no actual evidence of the reported gun shots."

One hand went up in the middle of the crowd.

"Gentleman in the yellow shirt ... what's your question?"

"How can you be sure about no gunfire? I mean, it's a huge area..."

"We canvassed the entire grounds. There was no evidence of a gun being fired. After extensive interviews with the concert goers and the food vendors, no one actually heard gunshots. We've determined the calls to 911 to be a hoax. Next!" she shouted for more questions.

A woman close to us thrust her arm in the air.

"After all the vandalism ... the theft ... and now gunshots, how are you guaranteeing our safety at this festival? Not only ours, but the attendees as well."

The officer explained how they'd added patrols and the hours monitored. Other than the one theft and a couple of random property damages, there wasn't evidence of widespread crime. It sounded to me like they blamed the damage that happened on our vendor row as a random act.

Yvette tried grabbing her partner's arms before her right hand shot up into the air. She failed, and Shelly shouted over our heads, "I want to know who is spreading lies about the safety of our product!"

My head dropped, and I heard Yvette gasp.

The officer didn't know how to answer that one, but asked Shelly to stick around and she'd get the details of her complaint.

I couldn't help but wonder if there was a connection between each of these festival disturbances. Or were they? And was the dog poisoning part of it, too? Who was sadistic enough to purposely poison dogs? Were the theft, vandalism, poisoning, and alleged gunfire all separate incidents, with no correlation among them? Seemed unlikely.

CHAPTER NINE

I stayed behind with Shelly and Yvette while they spoke to the officer. Of course, there was nothing the City of Mesa could do at this time. The FDA was looking into the matter and the Pupcakes owners would have to be patient as their investigation proceeded.

As we walked out of the city building, Yvette's phone rang. They had been summoned to their West Valley factory to meet the team of inspectors. Shadow and I wished them well and proceeded to the Dharma tent where we found Lexi talking with customers.

I glanced over at Pupcakes as we walked around to the side entrance of our own. It looked to me like they'd left a flap open. Not knowing whether they'd secured all their product before rushing off, I peeked inside. Shadow's nose immediately went into overdrive, and she pulled me all the way in.

"Shadow! This is trespassing!" I whispered, looking around at the empty shelving units. All the product was gone. Shadow yanked at her leash, causing me to whiplash in the opposite direction. "What is it?"

She led me to the far left-hand corner of the tent, sniffing intently all along the flooring. "C'mon, Shadow. There's nothing here and we need to get to work." I was more concerned that we didn't know what was making dogs ill. What if it was something dogs came into contact with at this booth? Dust they inhaled? I mean, Valley Fever was a real thing in Arizona. Could some dogs have come down with that? Seemed unlikely since veterinarians were familiar with those symptoms and could test for it. That Shelly and Yvette were told dogs were 'poisoned' seemed much more sinister.

Regardless, I pulled the leash to get Shadow's attention. That's when I saw what she was interested in. Under the bottom of the siding, I saw a flash of blue. I kneeled down, grabbing it just outside the booth's edge. Shadow squirmed and let out a small woof.

"Is this what you wanted?" I held up a plastic blue and white container of breath mints. "You can't have these!" Once I picked up the container, she became satisfied. I set the mints down on one of the empty shelving units, and she followed me out.

Lexi was finishing a shoulder massage when we walked inside our booth. I secured Shadow to her lead and she lapped up water from her bowl. After the customers left, I filled Lexi in on the last-minute meeting at City Hall, and how I was asked to help the Pupcakes owners with their mystery.

Laughing, she said, "You always seem to find yourself in the middle of drama, Libby!"

"Hey, I didn't bring this on!" I defended. "And what about my mother's place being robbed? I feel we should help her, too."

"We?" Lexi's eyebrows lifted.

"Well, okay, Shadow and me, I guess," I conceded.

"No. I understand—it's not like you asked to be involved in any of this. And it is probably better that we all put our heads together. Maybe we can help with some leads for the police to follow?"

"Yes! Exactly!" Then I remembered being reprimanded in the past for sticking my nose where it didn't belong. *Should I just stay out of this? Let the police do their job?* "What are you thinking?" I asked, seeing that my friend was concentrating intently on something.

"It's just something that JJ mentioned recently. The police force is awfully short-handed these days. Nowadays, things like petty theft—and that *is* how the Stitches of Love robbery will be classified—rarely receive any attention. I'm sure with the Pupcakes & More claim falling under the FDA jurisdiction, the local police won't be involved at all. Will the FDA even look into the specifics or only determine whether their manufacturing is safe?"

I nodded. Shadow whined. And both Lexi and I looked down at her. *Was she paying attention to our conversation?* Sure seemed like she was trying to tell us something. I looked up then and smiled; she was telling us we had company—Greg was standing there watching us.

"Hey! You left early this morning," I said, leaning over the counter and receiving a hug.

"Yeah, and now I'm heading up the mountain."

"Heber? Why?"

"I'll tell you more when I return tomorrow, but I couldn't get hold of you by phone and didn't want to leave town without you knowing."

I pulled my phone from my pocket. Sure enough, there were five missed calls.

"Oh, no. I'm so sorry. We were at City Hall … another incident …" I stopped. "Never mind. That's not important. I'm sorry I missed your calls. Everything alright?"

"Yes, yes … just fine. I have to run home for something. I'll stay the night and come back tomorrow. Call you tonight?" he asked, as he leaned over the counter and gave me a peck on the cheek. Then he was gone.

Lexi looked as confused as I was.

"That was strange, right?"

She nodded in agreement.

A customer walked up, and then I spent the rest of the morning busy with festival traffic. By the time Sydney and Diane arrived for their shift, I was definitely ready to be off my feet. Bella, Lexi, and I went to grab some noodle bowls for lunch and found a grassy area in the nearby park where we could take a break. Shadow stuck close; wherever food was, the Lab could be counted on to heel.

As we sat with our backs along a planter wall at the edge of the park, we listened to the bluegrass music being played and watched the people. Some were dancing, others were strolling by, and I saw a few sprawled out in the grass enjoying the midday sun with their eyes closed.

Bella chuckled at some kids playing, off to our right. "Hey, did you guys catch that fancy French lady earlier … I was watching her from our tent while she smelled different Zen Zone bath products."

Lexi and I looked at each other and shrugged. "Nope,

don't recall that one."

"Oh, I was thinking how some people get all dressed up for this event, and others barely make it out of their house with their loungewear on." She giggled. "Look, over there. Those teens, all in their fuzzy jammies! And over there, that guy's in a tuxedo. Oh wait, he's probably a performer. Hey, maybe that lady earlier was in some performance too? She was so put together, beautiful red silk outfit—what do you call those all-in-one thingies?" she asked, moving her hands from her torso down to her legs.

"A jumper or jumpsuit?" Lexi suggested.

"Yeah, a gorgeous silk jumper. Who'd wear that to a street festival?"

My phone ringing startled me. I grabbed it out of my pocket and answered.

"Shelly—how's it g—" I began to ask. "Uh, huh. Okay." I listened intently as her booming voice sped up, repeating everything the inspector had told them. "Well, that sounds positive, right?"

Lexi signaled to me, mouthing "Let's meet for dinner at my house … ask them to come…"

I nodded to her and waited for Shelly to take a breath. Once she did, I asked them over to Lexi's for dinner. The invitation thrilled them, and they became even more excited when they learned we would collaborate to support them. Of course, they mentioned we had to help my mom out as well.

Once I hung up the phone, I told Bella and Lexi that the Pupcakes & More booth would probably be cleared. We'd see them tonight to learn more.

"What a relief! So, I guess the inspection found nothing concerning?" Bella asked.

I shook my head. "Well, their manufacturing plant passed with flying colors. There are still tests to be done—both veterinary and the samples from the festival."

"Well, that sounds like it's progressing quickly, anyway. I pray their batches test negative and they can reopen."

I agreed. "Oh, and I told Shelly I'd text her the address and the time for dinner tonight. What do you think? Six? And, you're seriously not going to cook us dinner, right? Can I bring pizza or something?"

Lexi laughed. "No, I'm not cooking after working out here today. Sure, you bring pizza. I'll supply the wine. Tell Shelly and Yvette if they'd like anything else to drink, bring it. Six sounds good—that should give me time to get Joshua settled at his friend's house for the evening. Oh, and make sure to invite your mom and Margie … we need their input too."

We had a plan.

* * *

I accepted the glass of merlot from Lexi and offered to help her gather plates and such. She was reheating the pizza, so it was piping hot and told me everything else was ready. Shadow and I joined the others outside by the pool. Mom, Margie, and Bella were in deep conversation with Shelly and Yvette. The evening was stunning—perfect temperature. JJ came walking around the side of the house, carrying a couple more chairs.

"Hey, Libs!" he set down his load and greeted me with a giant hug. "This was unexpected, but so nice to meet everyone Lexi has been talking about. Also, good to see your mother—she's looking good!"

"Yeah—wish they'd had a better first day at the festival, but at least they've managed to put together some things and stay open. But, about that…"

"Oh, no … Libby, please tell me you will not get involved 'investigating'?" he chuckled.

I shrugged. "Nah, I don't think there's much I could do. But—"

"*But,* stay out of it, Libby. Let the police do their job."

"Will they, though?"

"Do their job? Of course. Why…"

"It's just—well, is this too petty for them to be concerned about?"

He considered. "It could be, Libby. But, if that's the case … maybe you should let it go, too?"

"Do you understand the proceeds benefit sick children?"

"I know. I know. Hey, let's just enjoy the evening, and all I'm saying is that I don't want you putting yourself in danger, or getting in trouble, for sticking your nose…"

"Ok. Got it." Disappointed, I turned away as my new friends walked up. *Ugh, JJ was always by-the-book. He could be so annoying that way.*

He set a chair out for me next to Yvette and I joined in on their conversation. Shadow nuzzled in between the two of us and I noticed how she kept glancing up at the woman. A couple times she let out a low woof.

I listened to all the theories that were being thrown around. Shelly considered a woman they had let go from the factory about a year prior—could she be causing problems now? Mom remembered a lady from the knitting group who suddenly stopped coming. Another friend in the group thought she may have said something to upset her. Would this be a cause for sabotaging their efforts at the festival? Seemed unlikely, but we were only brainstorming. No bad ideas, right?

Lexi called all of us over to the large outdoor dining table where she had just placed the three hot pizzas. "Come and get it while it's hot."

After consuming way too much, I asked the others if their businesses had gone through an inspection prior to being approved for a booth at the festival. They stared at me as though I'd sprouted horns. No, I learned Dharma Inspired Day Spa was the only business that Heather and Bailey visited, at least amongst this set of vendors. I wondered why that was. Then I explained how I was certain I'd seen Bailey, the assistant, the day before and she was rude, acting as though she'd never met me. Had it been months earlier, I'd understand her not remembering me. However, it was only one week ago. I felt unsettled about that interaction and couldn't place why.

"Maybe we should try again to ask around at the city office about those two?" Lexi suggested. Then she turned to her husband, "Hon, would you mind grabbing that pad of paper on the corner of the kitchen counter for me?"

He jumped up and went inside. Once he returned and handed the small notepad to her, she jotted a few things down.

"We should keep a record—all of you have had great ideas. So, keep brainstorming, and I'll scribe. So far—a lady from the knitting group. What was her name, Margie?"

"Caroline Krantz."

"And the woman you fired last year, Shelly? Her name was?"

"Dolores Ontiveros."

"Now, think a little bit … do you know where we'd find these ladies now?"

JJ stepped in. "Wait, wait. You ladies can't just show up at someone's door—especially someone you've fired—and start questioning them."

"Why not?" I asked.

"Ok, well, technically you *can* … but you probably won't get very far. And, you're opening yourselves up for more problems. Shelly, Yvette, you don't want a formerly terminated employee coming back to sue you for harassment or violating civil rights or anything."

Each of them seemed to consider that logic and nodded.

JJ continued. "Margie, Julia, in your case, I could see you trying to reach out to your friend out of concern because she never came back to the group. You could try locating her and ask her to come back to the knitting group. In the process, maybe you'd find out whether she even knew about your involvement with the hospital or with the festival."

I raised my hand.

JJ laughed. "Libby, this isn't school."

"I know. I just didn't want to be rude and interrupt." I smiled sheepishly. "I was thinking, maybe Shelly and Yvette can't reach out to their former employee, but what if I did? And of course, I'd never let on that I know them," I said, pointing to the ladies.

"What are you thinking?" Shelly asked.

"Well, do you know anything about her … a place she typically hangs out?"

They both answered simultaneously, "The dog park!" Then Shelly added, "Three Dog Park in Buckeye."

"Oh yeah, I forgot the factory's on the west side of town. Of course, she'd live over there too. Well, no matter, Shadow and I could venture over there and see if we run into her."

JJ piped up, "That's an awful long way to go, hoping to run into someone."

"She's *always* there on Sunday morning shortly after church this time of year," Yvette added.

"Ok. Well, my shift tomorrow at the festival is in the late afternoon. So, we'll head over to the park mid-morning and see what we learn. What type of dog does she have?"

"A Great Dane," Shelly answered.

"Okay … rarely see many of those around. Should be easy enough to spot."

I helped Lexi clear some plates while the rest of the group continued chatting. JJ took over as the scribe.

"While you're running around a dog park, I'll stop in at the city offices after my morning shift and ask around about those two ladies," Lexi offered. "The more I think about it, the more I don't like being singled out from all the vendors. I'd like to know more. I don't think I'll mention this to JJ though." She gave me a wink. We both knew him so well.

We quickly loaded the plates into the dishwasher. Lexi went to the refrigerator and pulled out a gorgeous lemon layered cake.

"When did you have the time to pull that together?" I asked.

"I didn't. But my neighbor did. She's the sweetest little lady—pops by now and then with the most decadent desserts. She's a fabulous baker."

"Well, I'm officially jealous. I'd love to have a neighbor

like yours!"

Between wine and cake and laughter, we managed to put the festival shenanigans behind us and enjoyed an evening among friends. The next thing I knew, it was already eleven o'clock.

"I'm sorry ladies, JJ, I've got to get to bed. This has been lovely and I look forward to finding the culprits." I pulled my chair back, and Shadow followed from underneath the table.

Lexi walked us out to the car.

"I hope they don't keep you up too much longer," I said as I hugged her goodbye.

"Oh, it's been so nice, though. I don't mind. See you tomorrow, Libby!"

CHAPTER TEN

When my phone rang the next morning, I was shocked to see the time because I had forgotten to set an alarm.

Groggily, I answered. It was Greg.

"Late night?" he asked.

"Actually, yes, it was," I answered, looking at my clock. "I can't believe it's already after eight."

"So, I guess you have the later shift at the festival then?" he asked.

"Yep. Hey, when are you headed back? And why the trip north again?"

He filled me in on the meeting with the Realtor, at the lot next door to my friend Sage's. It was a great deal, and he wanted to get the paperwork going, but there was information he couldn't readily retrieve on his laptop, requiring him to go home.

I listened to all the details about the property and his idea of it being an investment for now. If things worked out, maybe someday he'd build. He was willing to take his time before building, but he couldn't pass up this opportunity. Pleasantly relieved to have the pressure of future plans for us removed from his decision making, I realized that was all that had bothered me from our earlier conversation on this subject. I simply didn't want to be pressured or made to feel responsible for his large purchase if things didn't work out between us.

"So, you are heading back to the valley now?"

He confirmed he had one stop to make and then he'd see me later at the festival.

* * *

Shadow and I made the long drive across the valley to the town of Buckeye. Using GPS, we easily found Three Dog Park. It wasn't large; basically, it was a strip of land within a neighborhood, running along one of the community's main roads. I noticed there were only a few dogs and their people enjoying it. Lo and behold, one of them was a ginormous black and white Great Dane. The lady walking alongside the small horse-like dog was fairly tall, had brown curly hair, and looked like she'd just come from church. I guessed her age to be around late fifties, but I'm horrible at estimating ages, especially a woman's age.

I held tight to Shadow's leash, even though she really wanted off of it. As soon as we entered the gates, two small cattle dogs ran across the park and gave Shadow the once over. She barely paid attention to them, but only had eyes on the giant at the other end. That's when she started to pull me in that direction.

Before I knew it, the huge beast started running. In general, I'm not afraid of dogs. But, when you have one clearly larger than yourself, it makes you tense up. I saw Dolores running after and calling out loudly, "Tiny! Stop! Stop right now!"

I chuckled to myself. *Tiny. Too funny!* I made Shadow sit and she and I braced for what was coming. Hearing Tiny's owner shouting, "She's friendly ... really, she is!" I tightly held the leash with one hand and prepared my other hand in case it was needed. When the flash of black and white was within striking distance, she abruptly stopped and sat. Her head was easily at my shoulder level.

"Well, hello, Tiny ... you are a big girl, aren't you?"

She held up a paw, exactly at my height for shaking. Shadow whined and fidgeted.

"Shadow, be sweet. This is Tiny."

Both dogs looked each other over, but I was impressed that Tiny stayed seated until her owner arrived.

"I'm so sorry about that!" Dolores gasped, completely winded. "I know she's huge—that can be intimidating. She's a sweetheart, though. Oh, I'm Dolores—and I'm sure you know from all the ruckus that she's Tiny." The lady held out her hand to shake.

"Hi! I'm Libby Madsen and this is Shadow."

"Oh, she is so beautiful. I used to have a Lab—years back. Great dogs. I haven't seen you around here before."

"Just visiting, actually. My, uh, my brother."

Shadow and Tiny were circling us now, investigating each other further.

"Think it's okay for me to take Shadow's leash off

before she ties me up here?" I asked.

"Oh, sure. Tiny won't harm a flea. Promise."

I unsnapped the leash and the girls danced around each other a little … Shadow playing shy, and not understanding why she was no longer the largest one around.

"How long are you visiting?" Dolores asked.

"Just a few days. You live in this neighborhood?"

"Yep, nearly ten years now. Never thought I'd live this far west, but my job brought me here and well," her expression changed. "Well, things change, I guess."

"Oh. Where do you work?"

"The job that brought me to this part of the valley was Pupcakes & More. You may have heard of them? Now I'm at a different retailer's distribution warehouse down the road."

"Um, is that the dog treat—organic dog food, or something?"

"Yeah, that's it. Great dog food. I still feed Tiny their large breed food—it's great stuff."

"And you don't work there anymore?"

She hung her head. "Nah. I screwed up. Bad time last year when my mom died."

"Oh, no, I'm sorry."

"No, no … I'm getting through it now. I mean, I still have moments, but for months after her unexpected death, I couldn't even get out of bed in the morning." She looked across the way to where Tiny and Shadow had ventured together. "It was Tiny that saved my life. You know, you have to get them out of the house—there's no choice, you just do it. So, eventually I was able, and then each day I progressively got better. She definitely saved me. My mind was going to some dark places, I tell you."

I felt for her, remembering when my dad passed unexpectedly. Our family dog was such a comfort to me, too.

"So, were you let go from your job then?"

"Yeah. Totally my fault. I never called in and basically went missing for over a week. It's in the rules—you know, doctors note after three days, all that."

"Oh jeez. Seems like there'd be some leeway for grieving the loss of a parent."

"Honestly, I'm not sure I even told them a reason. I gave up on everything—so when I got the messages and eventually the termination letter, it did not surprise me at all. In fact, I was only surprised how long it took me to get that letter. I didn't want to work anymore. And hey, I am much better off today—much better job. My frame of mind has also greatly improved, and I have no complaints."

We both giggled as we watched the gentle giant and the retriever engage with the two other cattle dogs. The four were having a ball. I glimpsed the smile on Dolores' face—this was not Pupcakes complaimant. Nope, there had to be some other explanation.

I made a play by checking my watch. "Oh, look! I've got to get to work!"

"I thought you said you're visiting?"

"Uh, I mean … I've got to get my *brother* to work. He's lending me his car for the afternoon so I can drive to Mesa. There's a festival going on."

"Oh. I've never been to that one—heard it wasn't worth the drive over. There are better ones in the valley."

"Hmmm. Well, I'll check it out. Hey, it was nice meeting you! And Tiny. Hey, Shadow … c'mon!" I yelled out. "Let's go, girl." It took several calls, but finally Shadow reluctantly turned away from her newfound friends and came to me.

On our way back across town, I answered a call from Lexi using the hands-free technology in my 4Runner.

"Libby, I know your shift doesn't begin for a few more hours, but you need to get over here now. Are you still out in Buckeye?"

"I'm on my way back. I don't think my trip to the dog park helped solved who made the complaint against Shelly…"

Lexi cut me off. "Libby, never mind that. There are some officials here to talk to *you*."

"Oh. Why?"

"Zen Zone had some stuff stolen last night. Guess where they found it?"

"What? Another vendor theft?"

"Yeah, and this one has your name all over it. Just get here."

My heart skipped a beat; that got my attention. I drove straight to downtown Mesa.

After parking, I let Shadow out of the back seat and clipped her leash. We rushed to our booth, only slowing when I saw two police officers and the tall festival official turn away from Lexi and walk toward me.

"Libby Madsen?"

"Yes, how can I help you?"

"Libby, please come with us. We have some questions."

Before I knew what was happening, Lexi took Shadow from me, and one officer had me by the elbow, guiding me away. I looked back pleadingly over my shoulder and saw Lexi with her hand over her heart. From a distance, I also saw the once friendly hippie, John Piper, glaring at me.

"What is all this about?" I asked the officer walking

beside me.

She didn't answer; her eyes remained steadily ahead.

I turned to the festival official, who I noticed didn't have his ever-present bullhorn on him. "What's going on here?"

He also wouldn't answer.

Another officer who brought up the rear opened the door to the building, and they led me down a narrow hallway. We turned right, and then left again, and they placed me in a room with a table in the center. There were chairs on either side of the table. Other than that, it was a sterile-looking room—white laminate tile flooring, white walls, no windows. I noticed a camera in the upper left-hand corner of the room. I assumed from that we must be at the police station—only it appeared we must have entered it from a side or back entrance—as I hadn't recognized it as such from the outside.

"Am I under arrest for something?" I asked. "You know I get a phone call!"

The three who had escorted me here never entered the small room. The officer closed the door and I waited. After ten minutes, I remembered I still had my cell phone with me. I texted JJ:

Please recommend a lawyer and send to downtown Mesa! Hurry. Please!

Then, I sent one to Greg.

Please call and work with JJ to get me a lawyer. Police questioning me. Not sure what's going on.

I'd barely gotten the last text out when the door opened and the festival official and an officer walked in. Another officer brought in an additional chair, but then thankfully left for the three of us to have a conversation. It was getting quite claustrophobic in the small room.

"Libby Madsen, I'm Mr. Anderson. Mesa Arts & Crafts Festival Chair. We have reports that late last night, the vendor," he paused, flipping his notebook page over, "uh, Zen Zone, had product stolen. There's camera footage showing you—er, *allegedly* showing you—carrying a box of the stolen product from their booth. In another camera angle, that same person is placing the box into your storage container."

"That is ridiculous!" I shouted. "I was at a dinner party last night!"

The officer at the table asked, "What time were you at that party, Ms. Madsen?"

"Let's see … I picked up the pizza around five-thirty. I'm sure I got to Lexi's shortly before six. We were there for hours—I was the first to leave—it had to be eleven … maybe eleven-fifteen. I know I was home by eleven-thirty. She doesn't live far from me."

"Lexi? Full name, please."

"Alexis Johnson. She's my business partner and best friend. You were talking to her when I walked up to the booth a few minutes ago."

"Who else can corroborate your whereabouts?"

I listed off every person at the party. Alexis and her detective husband, Jeff Johnson, Isobel Crenshaw, Shelly Dunning, Yvette Garcia, Julia Madsen, and Margie. For the life of me, I couldn't remember mom's friend's last name.

"Who can verify the time you arrived home?"

My heart plummeted. No one.

CHAPTER ELEVEN

The door flew open about half an hour later.

A man I'd guess to be in his forties asked my interrogators, "Are you arresting my client?" When they stalled in answering, he came to my side and helped me up. "C'mon, Libby, we're leaving. Not another word."

He walked me through the labyrinth of hallways I assumed led to the front door. Nothing looked familiar.

"I'm Chris Manning. Jeff Johnson sent me to assist you. If you want, you can retain me as your attorney, or you're free to hire your own. Either way, I recommend you lawyer up. These guys mean business."

We turned another corner and walked out into the lobby. There were people at the counter and several seated in a waiting room style setup. That's when I saw my family—Greg, holding Shadow, along with Lexi and JJ, sitting in chairs patiently waiting for us. Shadow let out a bark and the rest of the group abruptly stood, rushing over.

"Libby! What's all this about?" Greg asked.

"I wish I knew." I gave him an enormous hug. Never was I so happy to see him and my friends.

Chris motioned for us to follow. We stepped outside of the building, moving around the corner and away from prying ears.

"Libby, they haven't brought charges yet. However, they suspect you of stealing product from a vendor at the festival last night."

I paced, barely able to contain my thoughts. "They were asking me all about my schedule last night. I was with them," I pointed to Lexi and JJ. "They can prove my alibi. I was nowhere near here."

"Yes, but it might not be enough. Think about the timeline of last evening carefully." He held up a folder of paperwork. "I'm going to read through this, and then I'll call you. That is, if you want to hire me as your attorney?"

I scrutinized the plump, short man with thinning hair for the first time. Forties may have been generous, but that didn't matter right now. He appeared pragmatic and reasonable, and I didn't have another attorney to call. "Yes. Yes, please. I did nothing wrong. In fact, we're trying to determine who stole from my mother—another vendor at the festival. And some new friends of ours as well, also vendors." I pointed in the general direction where our booths were located. "It seems to me I'm being framed. Probably for *all* the theft and vandalism, I don't know. None of this makes sense."

"There's been more theft? Vandalism?" he inquired.

"Yes! They didn't tell you about that, did they?" I remarked.

"Well, all of this has happened rather quickly, so no, I don't have a lot of information. Let me make a few phone calls, and I'll follow up with you by the end of the day. Promise."

Chris headed to the parking garage. We strolled back through the streets to our booth. As we passed by Zen Zone, I caught the looks cast from John and Jessica. Guess they were no longer new friends of ours. I knew better, but I sure wished I could talk to them. Why would everyone think *I* did this?

* * *

Greg went off to find us some food—I was famished.

When Yvette wandered over to our site fifteen minutes later, she pulled me into her arms. She was shocked to learn about another theft, and that the police had questioned me. I filled her in on what I knew about that, which was still very little. She glanced over at John down the lane, and I quickly grabbed her arm, and turned her to face me again.

"No, don't. I need no more trouble over there." Sighing, I moved slightly closer to her face, whispering, "And can we keep this between us for now? Shelly…"

She immediately understood and nodded. "Sure. Of course." We both looked over at her wife helping a customer at the front of their booth. She smiled widely. "Ohhh, she'd take out that hipster. Yeah, let's tell her another time."

I changed the subject, instead telling her all about my venture to the dog park and my meeting with Dolores.

I delicately relayed the part of the story about Dolores' excuse for her absences, trying to avoid a confrontation about that. Bottom line, I let Yvette know that was a dead end.

"I had no idea she'd lost her mother," she said, looking solemn.

"Well, if she never told you, how would you know?"

"True. I guess we never know completely what people are dealing with in their everyday lives, do we?"

That statement had me staring out over the lane toward Zen Zone Bathtime again. *Surely, John and Jessica weren't involved in setting me up, right? They couldn't be behind the other crimes going on, could they?* I couldn't be certain about anything at the moment, but Yvette was correct. It got me thinking—*what was happening in the lives of these criminals, which were now disrupting our lives? Why mess with innocent vendors at an arts and crafts festival?*

Yvette startled me. "There's a lot going on in that head of yours, Libby? What's up?"

"I'm thinking I must have gotten close to the culprit in all this. Otherwise, why accuse *me* of stealing bath bombs?"

She considered that for a second. "Good point. Also, why accuse *us* of poisoning dogs? Why go after our livelihood?"

Exactly. How were these connected? I questioned as my eyes scanned the row of craft booths. *And who would be the next victim?*

Mom called out, "Yoohoo!" and I whipped my head in her direction. "Anyone looking for these?" She held up some sunglasses. Shadow barked. "I guess Margie picked them up from somewhere, she doesn't remember where." As she got closer, Shadow jumped up and bumped mom's arm. The sunglasses fell.

"Shadow!" I yelled. "No! Sit!" Then, I turned to my mom. She brushed off her arm, but was fine.

Neither Yvette nor I recognized the glasses. I took them and told her I'd check with Lexi when she finished with her customer. Shelly summoned Yvette for help, so she left us. I realized Mom had mentioned nothing about their neighbors getting robbed. I invited her into the booth with me and filled her in on my morning at the police station.

I set the glasses on a nearby stack of boxes. Shadow immediately jumped up and knocked them off.

"What is going on with you, girl? Stop that!" I nudged her aside and picked up the dark glasses with wide black plastic frames. I set them high on another shelf. She sat and barked at them. "Oh, this is ridiculous." I took them down and let her sniff them all over. That seemed to satisfy her, and she finally settled down.

Mom gave me the update—they found the lady who had mysteriously left the knitting group. I'd known it was a longshot, but Caroline Krantz had no vendetta against anyone at Stitches of Love. She had explained to mom how her elderly sister in Kansas City needed help, so she had moved in with her. Caroline was hoping to one day move back to Arizona, but for now, she was needed in Kansas.

Another dead end.

* * *

The afternoon stayed quite busy and before we knew it, we were loading up our container with products again. Another successful day done, and it was the first time Lexi and I really had the chance to talk.

"So, Kathleen opened the container and a box of Zen Zone product was right inside?" I questioned. "That makes *no sense.*"

"I know. Exactly our thoughts, too. You and I have the code to the lock; Kathleen and Diane also have it. None of us know anything about how that box got inside."

"Wait. After the broken lock that first night, *who* replaced it?" I asked.

"JJ did."

"Dang it. I was hoping you'd say it was the festival people and we could start pointing fingers at them."

"Not so easily done. No, JJ went right out and bought a new one, only because he knew that'd be the fastest way."

"Guess we need to talk to Kathleen and Diane—did they give the code out to anyone else?"

"Yeah, I doubt it. We discussed where they were last night. Both have alibis and were far from downtown Mesa, but you're right. We need to learn if anyone else knew the code. I'll follow up with that."

"I still don't understand why they suspect it was me."

"I overheard Mr. Anderson saying something about 'footage'. I suppose they have something on camera?"

"But, Lexi, I was *not* here downtown last night. You know that."

"And, you went straight home, right?"

My eyebrows shot up. "Lexi! Of course, I did! I can't believe you'd have to ask."

"I know. I know. But, until they find out who really did it, you're going to have to answer hard questions."

"That's not a hard question. I was at home, in bed. Period."

"Okay." She patted my shoulder. "I'm sure we'll sort this out. Hey, how'd it go out at the dog park?"

I filled her in on that dead end and then remembered the sunglasses. We went back inside and I pulled them down from the shelf. Shadow started growling.

"Do you recognize these?" I asked Lexi.

"Nah. Definitely not my style. Where'd you find them—maybe a customer left them behind?"

"Mom only said Margie found them yesterday, but doesn't remember where."

"Hmm. Not mine, that's for sure."

I set them back on the shelf. Shadow let out one last woof as I picked up her leash and told her it was time to go home and find Greg.

CHAPTER TWELVE

Bella wasn't home when we arrived; I hadn't seen her all day. I wanted to learn more about whether she'd talked to her mom yet. Personally, I felt it would set her therapy back years. Since it wasn't my life, I needed to learn how to keep my ears open and my mouth shut. I'm sure she didn't need my advice. Unless she specifically asked for it.

Greg was sitting out back looking over some paperwork. "Well, hi there!" he said, as we came out the backdoor. Shadow rubbed against his legs and tried jumping onto his lap. "Whoa, girl. Not enough room up here, I don't think," he said chuckling, as he scurried to grab some papers before they fell to the ground.

"Whatcha doing?" I asked.

"Reviewing the real estate contract. Yeah, just making

sure that everything they told me yesterday was the same in print."

"Wow, that sure was fast."

"Right? I wouldn't mind going out there again before signing all this. Wanna take a little road trip? There's still lots of daylight left."

"Let's pick up some sandwiches at Subway and make it a little picnic, perhaps?" I suggested.

"Deal. Let me grab a few things. I'll drive."

The scenic drive on Main Street from Mesa to Apache Junction reminded me of a bygone era. There were still historic run-down motels from the days when this was the main highway into Phoenix. Some of those motels had investors attempting to restore them, others sadly did not.

"I can't believe you're thinking of buying in Apache Junction."

"Hey, it's gorgeous out here. I know you've been to Sage's lots of times. Tell me you don't see the beauty all around."

I laughed. "I know, I know. Where she lives is stunning." My eyes roved to either side of the Apache Trail, which is what the street name turns into once you've crossed into Apache Junction. All the dilapidated businesses and the ever-growing homelessness—it made me sad. "It's a great historic town—Sage has told me many stories since she moved out here. She loves the old western feel that is still so prominent. And she says everyone is so friendly here, and how it's maintained that small-town feel. I'm only sad about the increasing drug and homelessness problems, I guess."

"That's anywhere these days, Libby."

"I know. Unfortunately."

We turned off the Trail and proceeded to Goldfield Road. From there, we took a series of smaller dirt roads that eventually led to our destination: Quail Lane. We pulled to the side while a couple of horses and their riders passed us.

"You're right—the wild, wild west, alive and well," Greg said in his best western drawl.

"Such a goofball," I teased.

I admired Sage's house, which I saw off to our left as we drove past. To the right, we saw the most amazing late afternoon views of the Superstition Mountains. The late day sun lit them up in golden hues, with deep shadows in the canyons causing dramatic effects. Greg drove to the very end of the road, pulled off, following a couple of tire tracks through the lush desert. He turned off his Tundra, and Shadow stood up in the back seat, whipping her tail around, excited to explore.

"Better keep the leash on her for a bit until we're able to scope out what critters are lurking."

"Good idea."

I grabbed the Subway bag, got out and opened the back door, and quickly snatched up Shadow's leash before she jumped out. Greg pulled a couple of camp chairs and a little folding table from the bed of his truck, while I walked Shadow around to scout out the area. We were approximately two acres north of Sage's property at the end of the road.

"You said this property is five acres?" I asked Greg.

"Yep—it's a bit rectangular." He started walking west, and we followed him. The terrain was quite rocky, but also filled with desert sage with beautiful yellow blooms. Abundant mesquite and Palo Verde trees grew wild throughout.

"See that fence line there?" he asked, and I nodded. "That's state land beyond it—all the way to Highway 88. Nobody can build anything there. So, Sage's house, and the one behind hers, those will be the only neighbors. The one across the street east over there," he pointed toward the mountain, "they are snowbirds, I learned. Only here in the winter months."

I looked back toward the vast mountain range, then scanned the others in the distance: Four Peaks and the Goldfields. So gorgeous—It was perfect. I felt the tingle of butterflies in my stomach and for the first time, I could picture living here one day.

"I love it!"

"Good! Because I'm buying it!" he smiled, then leaned over and gave me a kiss. "Shall we go eat our dinner, Ms. Madsen?"

"We shall," I giggled.

As we walked back across the desert, I had a twinge of guilt over having been so petty previously about his desire to move to the valley. I really needed to work on that. Learn to go with the flow and not assume everyone was out to take my independence away from me. Or was it really about being afraid of the man who would take the sacred place in my heart that only my dear father had held? *Till now.* Yep, I had some growing up yet to do—I'd get there.

Shortly before I finished my sandwich, my phone rang. I saw it was Chris Manning. I sighed loudly, rolling my eyes. Greg shot me a questioning look.

"Just when I had put the world behind me out here in the desert, it's all caught up to me now." I offered as explanation and then pushed the button to answer. "Hello, this is Libby."

I watched Greg's eyes as they sought answers from my conversation. His eyebrows lifted, then fell. The frown lines appeared, then the smile lines would emerge. By the time I got off the phone, he was eager to hear how it went.

"Sorry, I was afraid if it was on speakerphone, the breeze would make it difficult to hear, and I didn't want to miss a single word."

Eagerly rolling his hand as though to speed things up, he prompted, "Yes, about that ... what did he say?"

"I guess the good news is that he feels confident charges *won't* be filed. He said they have some camera footage, and although the person has a similar build to mine, he could not see details. The prosecutor would be hard-pressed to prove anything based on that alone."

"So, I guess that gets us to the bad news, then?"

"Unfortunately, yes. The fact that possession is nine-tenths of the law and they found the goods within our container—that's not good. However, he assured me they'd have a hard time proving *I* stole anything. As he pointed out, why would I go to the effort to steal and then stash the stuff where it would so easily implicate me? It reeks of a setup. Or a truly stupid criminal."

He laughed at that. "I heard you going over the timeline—had he talked to the others yet to corroborate that?"

"Yeah, unfortunately, Bella hadn't seen either Shadow or me and couldn't say one-hundred percent whether my vehicle was in the garage when she arrived home that night.

She never looked in there and assumed I was in bed asleep; she arrived home around twelve-thirty."

"Hon, I tried calling you from eleven to somewhere after eleven-thirty and I only got voice mail. You know I'm going to be questioned eventually as well."

"I know. I wish I'd had my sounds on—that would make all of this verifiable, if I'd answered. Isn't there some way for them to see which cell tower my phone pinged from? They will not find it downtown Mesa that night, I assure you of that."

He shrugged. "In the movies, they do it that way all the time. Not sure how it goes in real life, though."

We gathered our empty sandwich wrappings when Shadow abruptly stood and barked. Someone was walking down the road toward us.

"Oh look, it's Sage!" I said, grabbing Shadow's leash and walking toward my friend. "Hi there!"

When she reached us, she enveloped me in a warm hug. "So good to see you. Did he do it?" she asked, pointing her chin in Greg's direction.

"I think he's going to."

"You're going to be my neighbor?" she exclaimed.

"Well, hold on ... not sure about that. But I think Greg is buying the property as an investment, at least."

She gave me a sly, disbelieving smile. "You'll be my neighbor. Trust me." She winked, and we walked over to Greg. "It's gorgeous this time of day, isn't it? If this doesn't convince you to buy, I don't know what else would."

"Oh, it's really a simple decision. The location is perfect, and I was quite surprised at the price. Thought it would be a whole lot more, honestly."

"I'm thrilled!" She clapped her hands together. "I've

been so worried about who would buy and end up building right next to me. I mean, could you imagine if they ended up blocking my view here? A huge two-story, or an enormous garage or something?"

Greg chuckled. "I don't think I'll be building for some time, but I promise I'd consider how it'd affect your property when I do. Here, let's walk up this way and I'll show you what I was initially thinking."

I glanced at my watch. I wanted to get home and talk to Lexi, but I was equally interested in hearing Greg's plans. Shadow pulled at the leash and we followed, along what looked to be a small game trail. The terrain gradually sloped into a natural wash before we climbed up the other side to the highest point on the property. Looking out over the desert, back toward the mountain, Sage's home was southeast from here.

"I think the main house should go here—the access would be from this road—what is it? Coyote Run." He turned and pointed behind us, to the southwest. "Over there, it's all state-owned land north and west from the property line here. Now, east of here, on the other side of the wash, and closer to Quail Lane, I could see a guest house, perhaps someday. Mother-in-law quarters?" He looked at me cautiously as he mumbled that last part.

"Greg, it's perfect!" Sage exclaimed.

"And see, I don't think this affects any of your views, does it?" he asked.

"None."

"Mother-in-law quarters?" I questioned. "You really want Julia living here? Or are you talking about your mom?"

Laughing, he said, "Whoever wants to come visit us? Or whoever is in need and wants to stay. Doesn't matter."

He leaned over and kissed the top of my head.

"Oh, you two are *so cute*," Sage cooed. "I can't wait until we're neighbors!"

* * *

Back at home, I immediately called Lexi. I was eager to learn more.

She had talked to both Diane and Kathleen, and as we thought, neither of them had given the container's lock code out to anyone else. Lexi confirmed that an investigator had reached out to her, and she walked them through the previous evening's timeline and accounted for seeing me at her home from slightly before six and until shortly after eleven.

When I told her about my call with the attorney, she also became confident that we would resolve everything soon. Bella walked in then and I said goodbye to Lexi.

"Have you heard the latest?" Bella asked as I hung up.

"What?"

"I hung around the festival to hear the band playing … and, as I was leaving, I learned they found your mom's stolen goods!"

"That's great! Where?"

"Not sure. Don't know all the details."

I scrolled through my phone and selected my mom on my contact list.

"Libby!" she answered. "They found our stuff!"

"I just heard. Where'd they find it?"

"Oh, some candlemaker's booth a row behind ours. In fact, you can easily walk from ours to the back of their tent."

"And the police didn't search there initially?"

"They said they did. And the gentleman selling candles was sure the bag wasn't there even earlier in the day today!"

"Okay, that's strange. Someone is stealing from vendors and then *bringing stuff back*, leaving it at other booths? None of this makes sense."

"That's what the nice police officer said as well. Pranks."

I thought about that for a moment. I'm sorry, but after the police questioned me and when I felt I was about to be arrested, that didn't exactly seem like a prank to me. Hopefully, they would vindicate me and find the punk kids that were causing trouble. For now, I was content leaving mom thinking pranks were going on so she wouldn't worry anymore. I was happy my mom and her friends had retrieved their stolen items.

"It was also nice to see that not all the product was damaged—I went through it all, and there's still much we can sell. With what the ladies were currently knitting, plus the recovered pieces, the donations should be pretty substantial. What a relief!"

I tried to get a word in, but she continued right on.

"Hey, I just heard from Kathy. You know, the one you met from Just Ducky? She was so distraught over what had happened that she banded together her knitting group in Tahoe and said she's just sent us a package—overnight delivery. We'll have so much to sell for the rest of the week!"

"That's fantastic!" I got in just between breaths before she continued.

"Oh! And, Libby, you'll never believe who was hanging out around our booth this evening?"

"Who?"

"Trixie—or, Violet. Whatever her name is. I *know* it was her."

Chills ran the length of my spine. I had been certain my mom was wrong earlier when she'd mentioned Violet. Now I couldn't help but wonder if that woman from our past was stalking us again. Was she behind the festival thefts? It made little sense, but then again, the actions of criminals—do they *ever* make sense?

CHAPTER THIRTEEN

Shelly's phone call came almost the instant I ended the conversation with my mother.

"Hey, join us for Sunday roast down at the pub," her voice was as boisterous as usual, almost startling.

I looked over at Greg; he and Shadow had settled into their places on the sofa. Bella had just come home and was offering me a glass from the bottle of wine she'd opened.

"Uh, looks like we're kind of ..."

"Oh, c'mon Libby ... grab that handsome guy and your roommate and let's make a party of it. We'll be outside and the pub is dog friendly—bring Shadow." I could hear Yvette whoop and holler in the background, and I wasn't sure I was exactly in the party mode. "No, seriously, Libby, we wanted to give some updates. I think we're on to something—at least where it pertains to our dog poisoning case. And, I'm very curious to learn more about your involvement at Zen Zone."

My heart skipped; it was silly to think that Yvette could keep that secret long. I turned and asked Greg and Bella. They hadn't been to this particular pub, so they were eager.

Walking across the parking lot, I could already hear Shelly's voice. We found the gate and entered the patio, easily finding our friends at the other end. As we approached the table, I realized John and Jessica from Zen Zone were sitting with them, and butterflies fluttered around in my belly.

John stood up and approached me. Shadow let out a low woof. "Don't worry, Libby. I know there's more to the story, and we're here to get a beat on the real story. Man, I'm sorry I was quick to judge earlier."

Reaching my hand out to shake his, I explained, "I swear, John. I am not responsible for the theft."

He pulled me in closer for a hug. "I know. And I'm sorry again—I should have known from the start. Now, we all need to figure out who is messing with our businesses."

Greg shook his hand. Bella said hi to everyone, and Shadow made her way around the table, getting love from each person before she settled in underneath my chair. I scanned the group, realizing there were more empty place settings.

Yvette nudged me, and I accepted when she offered to fill a pint from the pitcher sitting near her. She leaned in and whispered, "I'm sorry. Shelly got talking to John earlier, I didn't…"

I waved her off. "No need to explain. Really. It's fine."

Lexi and JJ walked up then. "Hey!" she said. JJ took a seat by Greg and Lexi sat across from me, next to Bella.

"So, let me guess … my mom and Margie are the next to arrive?" I questioned.

Yvette chuckled. "We invited everyone, yes. I'm not sure if they're able to join or not."

John asked the server to load the table up with appetizers, another pitcher of beer, and then turned his attention back to the rest of us.

"Hey, folks, so righteous we could gather like this, so we got us some munchies to start on. Cool."

Jessica smiled, and then in her soft voice that had us all leaning in closer, she asked, "Shelly, will Pupcakes open again tomorrow at the festival? What's the latest?"

We sat back in our chairs, easily able to hear Shelly's answer. "Still not sure. But we're extremely hopeful to be back before it's all over. I can't remember who all I've told …" she continued to relate the story about the inspector's report from their factory.

As she spoke, I observed Lexi's attention being diverted elsewhere. I turned my head to see. Inside, the restaurant was busy, and I strained to see beyond the reflection of the outdoor patio lights. She saw me looking and shrugged, questioning. I'd ask her later.

Tuning back into the group's conversation, John was telling us about something he'd overheard earlier in the day.

"Yeah, man, their voices sounded angry. One definitely said 'they're up to it again' … but you know, it was hard to hear much."

"Did you walk in anyway?" Shelly asked.

"Oh, for sure. Our merch was taken—I needed to know what they were doing! So, I walked on in. Acted like I hadn't heard a thing." He shook his head and scoffed. "Oh man, they were nervous. Whatever they were talking about came to an abrupt halt. I definitely interrupted *something*."

"What did you learn?" Greg asked. "About the theft?"

John glanced nervously at me, then back at Greg. "Dude, they are certain they've caught their suspect." His gaze dropped to the table.

"What did they tell you?" I asked. "Specifically."

He hesitated for a second, then leaned in, resting his elbows on the table. We all followed suit and learned again that they had camera footage. Then he shared that the police have physical evidence as well. My stomach lurched. *Why hadn't my attorney mentioned that part?* I forced myself to listen and not become distracted.

"Did they say *what* physical evidence they'd found?" I quietly asked.

"They wouldn't share specifics, Libby." Again, his gaze went to the table. He appeared shamed about the whole thing.

Shelly added, "Unless it ties to Libby's DNA—they ain't got shit!"

With her arm already around Shelly's shoulders, Yvette lightly patted her back. "I'm sure all this will get figured out soon enough. Now, John, do you have any ideas who may have done it?"

He and Jessica both shook their heads.

Lexi commented, "I wonder what they meant by 'they're up to it again'? I mean ... wonder if that's related to the thefts? Has this type of thing happened before?" Then she turned to her husband. "Babe, is this something you might be able to help with? Just ask around the station?"

JJ shrugged. "I'm not sure I'll learn anything since it's

not my case. But, of course, let me see what I can do."

I thanked him and as uneasy as I was, it gave me comfort to have friends looking out after me.

Yvette piped up, answering Lexi's earlier question. "I think it could mean there was another hit. Another vendor stolen from ..." she paused, as two servers moved in and began setting platters down the center of the table.

Everything smelled delicious. There were the typical bar food appetizers: wings, fried mushrooms, and loaded potato skins. The plates that caught my eye, however: miniature shepherd pies, fish 'n chip bites, and an enormous charcuterie board. Greg and I had the same thought, and we both asked the server for a Guinness. We dove right into the English platters first.

Between bites, I asked Yvette about the dogs that were ill. I already knew that they didn't know who the victims were, but I wondered perhaps if they named a veterinarian in the paperwork. She thought about it for a minute and couldn't remember, but said she'd follow up when she got home. I suggested that if we could learn where even one dog was treated, maybe I could take Shadow there and we could do some sleuthing. Of course, all Shadow heard was her name, so she was certain that meant food was about to be delivered to her at floor-level any moment.

Once we finished all the appetizer platters, a server approached our table and inquired if we were prepared to order entrees. There wasn't a single hungry person at the table; those were hearty appetizers.

I leaned toward Lexi when I saw her looking inside the restaurant again. "What do you see in there?"

She shook her head. "I'm not sure. I could have sworn I recognized someone—and that they kept staring outside at us. This is baffling, though. As you can see, there's no one there!"

"I'm sure you're not seeing things. Let's use the restroom … look around."

We excused ourselves and headed inside.

From when we first arrived over an hour ago, the place had cleared out considerably. There were several booths occupied and about five tables in the center of the room. The bar area had three people on stools. Lexi looked among the patrons as we passed through the building to the restrooms at the far end. As soon as we stepped inside the ladies' room, she shook her head.

"Yep, it's official. I'm losing my mind."

"Well, it doesn't mean whoever you saw hadn't already left. Who did you think you saw?" I added, as I opened a stall and went in. Lexi went into another one of the four stalls.

"You know, I'm not entirely sure. Seemed familiar though."

Just then a toilet flushed and a couple seconds later a stall door opened and from underneath my door, I saw thick-heeled black boots pass by. I thought we were the only ones in the bathroom—*why hadn't I checked the other stalls?* The water ran at the faucet, then the automatic paper towel dispenser, and the door opened and closed.

"Did you see the boots?" I whispered.

"Shhh." Lexi was quick to shush me.

We both finished and washed our hands. Lexi tiptoed toward the last stall and bent down to look for feet.

"I had no idea anyone was in here," she finally said.

"I know! But, did you see those boots?"

"No. What boots?"

"Whoever walked out had on those combat-style black boots."

"And is that supposed to mean something to me?"

"We've seen someone recently who wears that style. I'm sure we have—maybe we *are* being followed."

We hurried through the door and out into the restaurant. Scanning the entire restaurant, we caught the front door closing and what looked to be a woman about my height who'd just gone through. I rushed toward the door, and Lexi followed me. We pushed our way through the glass door in time to see a Denali speed away.

"Well, that could have been anyone. Honestly, what are we thinking?" Lexi began laughing, and that got me started, too.

"We're so dumb. How much have we had to drink anyway? A lady going to the bathroom at the same time as us, and *that's* suspicious?" I busted out again laughing.

We went back to the patio in time to find the rest of the group gathering their things. Greg and JJ looked at us wearily, noticing we were suppressing laughter.

"What are you two up to?" JJ asked.

We couldn't answer him. All we did was laugh at our antics. *Chasing a woman from the building? What were we thinking?*

CHAPTER FOURTEEN

After our night out at the pub, the early morning alarm was, well, alarming. Ugh. Suddenly, a week-long festival was taking its toll. Or was it actually an impending arrest that was zapping my energy? I'm sure both were, at this stage.

I grudgingly got out of bed and immediately into the shower, hoping hot water would jolt me into existence. It helped, but coffee would be the remedy. I tied my robe around my waist and made my way to the kitchen, where I found Bella had already started it. Bless her.

"Are you opening the booth this morning?" she asked.

"Yep—guess you and I are the openers, huh?" I pulled out a stool and sat, waiting for the coffeemaker to finish.

"And Greg starts his big first day at the desk, doesn't

he?" She laughed as she pulled down a couple of mugs from the cabinet above.

"Yeah, should be interesting. To my knowledge, he's never had a desk job before. I give it a day before he's bored out of his mind!" The image of the always-on-the-go forest ranger stuck in an office was actually quite frightening. I hoped he wouldn't have to do that for too long. *Or did I? It would keep him here in town.*

My phone buzzed on the countertop. I looked at the time on the microwave; not even seven, who the heck was calling so early? I flipped the phone over and saw it was Chris Manning, my attorney.

"Wow, you've got an early start to your day."

"Oh, is it too early? I was hoping to catch you before you left for downtown."

"You caught me. Now what?"

"Well, if possible, I was hoping I could meet you on the front steps at the courthouse. They are going to share the camera footage with us."

Why did I feel this was a setup?

"Chris, I'm not being arrested today, am I?"

"No. No, Libby. I arranged for us to view the evidence the prosecutors have gathered. That's it—I promise."

"I have the early shift at the festival. How long will this take?" Bella was motioning in the background that she could handle the opening.

"It won't take long, Libby. They have little evidence—that's exactly the point, and what we need to see for ourselves."

I mouthed to Bella, *are you sure?* She nodded and I confirmed I could meet Chris at eight.

* * *

When I followed the sidewalk out of the parking garage and rounded the corner of the courthouse building, I saw Chris standing exactly where we agreed. He led me into the already bustling hall of justice. A tingle threaded its way down my arms. I realized once caught up in this system, there was little one could do except trust. Trust that you have a good lawyer. Trust the witnesses and judges. And, God forbid, hope you never reach the point where a jury of your peers decides your fate.

As I was gathering my sweater and my purse from the security conveyor belt, I watched the diverse cross section of our society filing into the nearby jury selection room. Thankfully, we weren't at that stage yet where this was even a possibility for me, but as we passed by and continued down a long hallway, I reflected on what I'd seen already. Several older people, dressed dutifully and ready for action. Many young folks whom I would guess don't even remember their recent civics lessons. Nearly all of them appeared as though they would rather do *anything* but sit in court all day for jury selection.

Chris opened a door and stood aside as I crossed the threshold. It was a small, cold room—much like the interrogation room I'd been in a couple of days ago, over at the police station. I took a seat, and he wrangled with the audio-video equipment. After some white noise, a grainy nighttime image of a booth came into view.

"Wait. Can you pause it?"

Chris punched a button on the remote. I stood and moved closer to the screen.

"Is this Zen Zone?"

"Hard to tell, huh?"

I nodded and motioned for him to continue.

"Okay, there's the sign. It is. Oh, look!" I pointed to a dark figure that had emerged from one corner and slunk around the front until it disappeared into the darkness on the other side. I waited for more.

"Looks like that's it on this camera," he said.

"That's it?" I asked, laughing. "You can't tell *anything* about the person from that footage! Do *you* think that looks like me?"

"No. And that's exactly why we're here. Maybe there's something that will stand out—mannerisms, or *something* you may recognize from someone else you've seen at the festival."

He selected another file using the remote control. I sat back down, waiting as he fumbled around with the technology. As soon as the new image popped up on the screen, I recognized it immediately as the back end of our Dharma Inspired booth. The lighting was better in this video—I suspected there must be a street lamp close by, even though I'd never paid attention to that detail.

"Oh, crap!" My heart flip-flopped and I jumped up. "That *is* me."

* * *

I called Bella to make sure she was okay at the booth on her own for another hour or so. I had to run home and get Shadow, but also my stomach continued to lurch. As I drove the city streets, the video images ran through my head. My lawyer assured me it was very easy to discredit. That hadn't made me feel any better.

Struggling to remember what I was stuffing into the

container and *when*, my stomach wouldn't stop rumbling. *It couldn't have been that night of the theft! I did not drive downtown to the festival. There's no way.* I turned onto my street and hurriedly parked in the driveway.

I unlocked my front door, let Shadow out of her kennel, and immediately took her outside into the backyard. I felt the vibration of the phone in my front pocket.

"Mom—hi!"

"I was worried when I saw Bella alone at your booth. Are you okay?"

"Uh, yeah," I hesitated. "Yes. Everything will be fine."

"Sorry I missed you last night. It was going to be too late for me to join—but Bella filled me in."

"Oh, right." I'd nearly forgotten all about our night out at the pub. "At least John doesn't suspect me any longer. But—"

"What is it, Libby? You sound distracted."

"I met with my lawyer this morning, and I've seen the video of the Zen Zone theft."

"Could you tell who it was?"

"No, not at all. At least, not the footage at their tent. The person is covered head to foot in black—hoodie, mask, everything. No way to see their face. Chris says that works in my favor."

"I feel there's a *but* coming…"

"Well, yeah … there's clear video of me putting something into our container."

"Oh…"

"It wasn't me, Mom!"

"I know. I know, hon."

"Chris pointed out there was no date and time—at least in the footage we saw." I turned to Shadow and snapped my fingers, calling her back into the house.

As I wrapped up my phone call with my mom, I gathered a few items I needed to take with me and got Shadow ready as well. By the time I ended the call, I had Shadow loaded into my 4Runner, and off we went.

It was a sunny Monday morning and the festival crowd was light. I had wondered how a week-long festival would work out, seeing that many people would work during the weekdays. By mid-morning, I realized Arizona's winter visitors made up most of our customers. During lunchtime, there were even more of them and downtown workers on their lunch break.

John sauntered over to our booth during a lull after lunch.

"Man, we had a great morning. How about you guys?"

"Not bad. Better than I thought it'd be."

Shelly heard our voices, apparently, and came out to join us. We learned Yvette was out picking up some food for them. For the first time all day, I actually felt hunger. Since my shift was almost over, I knew I could get something to eat soon.

Lexi and Sydney walked up not long after I'd had that thought.

Sydney pointed east of where we were. "Did you see that commotion?"

All of us shook our heads.

"They were chasing someone down. Sheesh! What's going on around here?"

I asked, "The police were chasing someone?"

Lexi nodded, rolling her eyes. "I swear, it feels as though blatant theft has become a staple in our society, hasn't it?"

"Do we know that's what happened?"

"I guess not. But still…" Lexi handed Sydney a box of candles and lotions and the young girl went inside to get the shelves restocked.

"How'd it go with your lawyer?" Lexi asked me, changing subjects.

The other vendors turned their eyes on me, also expecting to hear the update. I filled them in, and the sentiment seemed to be the same. It made us all question whether we'd sign up for this again next year. If the officials couldn't keep us safe, we'd take our business elsewhere. It wasn't long before everyone was called back to duty as customers arrived at their booths.

On my way out, Shadow and I ran into Yvette with her arms full of takeout containers. I helped her with the load by taking the drinks.

"Thanks, Libby. I've been trying to find a time to call you this morning," she mentioned. "I've got some information for you."

We arrived at their booth and snuck in through the back flap. I set the drinks down on the first empty surface I found. Once she placed her load on the table, too, she reached into her pocket.

"These are the two veterinarians I saw listed on the inspector's report. Although the inspector's report did not mention the complainants by name, it noted the breeds of dogs. One was a boxer. And, uh, I believe one went to this vet here," she said, pointing to the paper she handed to me. "I hope you can read my writing. The other breed was a cocker spaniel."

"Okay, perfect. Shadow and I will see what we can learn." We said our goodbyes and were on our way.

As we pulled into the parking lot at the first veterinarian's office in Tempe, I noticed few cars in the parking lot. Shadow's ears were pressed against her head when I opened the back door to let her out.

"Oh, my poor girl," I quietly said, trying to coax her. "I promise lots of cookies once we get home. Yvette and Shelly need your help right now—let's go!" Her ears had perked up with the promise of a treat. However, she only reluctantly jumped down and followed me inside.

Even though this was not her normal doctor's office, her nose knew the smells all the same. She kept close to my side while we waited in line. Even the cute cocker spaniel in front of us didn't distract Shadow from her nervousness. I overheard the lady ask the spaniel's owner if Lady was still experiencing vomiting since their first visit. She said no. Poor little pup.

When it was our turn, I filled out paperwork and talked with the nice lady at the front desk, while Shadow couldn't take her eyes off of Lady sitting across the waiting room now. Soon Lady was led into a room and Shadow huddled even closer to me. Her fear never waned—even thirty minutes later once we were situated in an exam room, she hid under the chair I sat in.

The technician who walked into the room was a young spritely woman with her long brown hair tied up into a bun on the top of her head.

"Good morning," she said, and then reading from the clipboard, "is this Shadow?" She kneeled down and peered at the black Lab cowering behind my legs. "Hey, sweetie. I think I have something you might like." She stood and opened a container, pulling out a treat.

Shadow's nose peeked out first as she crept from

beneath the chair.

"There we go. What a good girl!" the technician exclaimed as she hid the treat then took Shadow's leash and addressed me. "It's a dirty trick, I know. I won't give her anything until we determine what's making her tummy sick." She guided Shadow over to a large platform, which functioned as a scale and an examination table. Using a pedal for the hydraulic lift, she raised the table off the ground a couple of feet.

I had momentary guilt about lying.

"Yeah, I've been worried. We've been out at the arts festival..." I immediately saw her flinch. "What—have you been there, too?"

She shrugged her shoulders. "No, but you were saying?"

"Oh, right ... anyway, we bought some organic dog treats out there." I reached into my purse and pulled out the package. "These—" I held them up and saw her look of recognition. "Have you tried these before? I've heard good things. But yesterday I started hearing a rumor about how they've made other dogs sick. Now I'm worried."

"What are Shadow's symptoms?"

"Um, she hasn't actually thrown up yet. I'm trying to be proactive, though. Have you treated any of the dogs who got sick?"

She didn't respond immediately, but used her stethoscope to listen to the patient's heartbeat. Then, she took her temperature. "We have seen some very ill dogs recently. But the good news is that all of Shadow's vitals are great. Let's see what the doctor has to say—she may want to draw some blood. We'll see."

With that, the technician lowered the table and handed Shadow back over to me and left through the door. Shadow seemed pleased and less stressed now.

"See, nothing to worry about, sweet girl!" I petted her, and she sat on my feet.

Looking around the sterile room with pictures of cats and dogs on all the walls, I homed in on the heartworm diagram that showed the progression of that awful disease. Hearing voices from the other side of the door—the one that led to the inner workings of the medical facility and not the lobby—I found new interest in a feline leukemia chart hanging on that door.

"Why would she be asking about other pets?" I heard an unfamiliar woman's voice ask.

I couldn't hear anyone answer that question, so I assumed she must be on the phone.

"I don't know, but somehow she knows they received treatment here!"

My pulse quickened.

Everything slowed.

I heard rummaging around and a couple of other distant voices. Then, the woman's voice again.

"Of course, we will not give her information. How stupid do you think I am?" she spat, then slammed the phone down.

I whirled around to get back to my seat. "Shadow!" I whispered. "C'mon!" She sauntered back over to me, much more relaxed than earlier.

No footfalls came near the door. As my eyes roved around the room again, I noticed there were several clipboards sitting in a basket on the edge of the countertop. They appeared to have paperwork attached.

I couldn't help myself; I quietly tiptoed over and glanced. Sure enough, each held patient paperwork. The basket they were in was labeled: **To Be Recorded**

I listened for a moment. Everything was quiet, except for sounds coming from the lobby and some distant voices in the medical rooms.

My fingers lifted each record and my eyes scanned the dog breed. Two charts down in the pile, I saw a cocker spaniel—Lady. It was the dog that had been ahead of us in line! I thumbed through, reading what I could quickly, and keeping an ear tuned for anyone approaching.

I saw the words Pupcakes & More, and festival, and organic treats. This was one of them! Frantically scanning, I grabbed my phone from my pocket and selected the camera icon. Just before snapping the third picture, I heard a door slam and our technician's voice.

"Room 3, Doctor," she said.

My hands fumbled the phone, and it went sliding across the floor. The clipboard slammed down into the basket, nearly spilling over onto the floor.

Shadow barked.

I'd barely made it into my seat when the door opened. Both the doctor and the technician looked around the room in amusement. I smiled at them and Shadow gave a little whine before slinking back under the chair. I felt sure they heard the ruckus.

"Hello, I'm Dr. Paula Fanter. Oh, just call me Paula—we're quite informal around here." She smiled widely and appeared friendly enough.

During the doctor's introduction, the technician used her techniques to get her hands on Shadow again. I wondered if she'd find my phone under there somewhere. My eyes gave a quick scan of the room and I couldn't figure out where it had landed.

"So, I hear you're concerned your dog may have been poisoned?" she asked me. "But, she's not showing any symptoms?"

"Uh, well … last night I got worried when she wouldn't eat dinner. Other than that … uh, no. As I was telling your tech, we'd been at a festival where we learned some other dogs became ill."

"And she's completely up-to-date on vaccinations? Has she been seeing another veterinarian?" she asked, as she flipped through the pages. "You are new to our clinic, right?"

"Yes. Yes, she's had all her shots. I just couldn't get her into her regular doctor today and someone recommended we come here."

Dr. Fanter looked up from the paperwork with a grin before turning her attention to Shadow on the table. The technician moved aside, and that's when I saw her look questioningly at the basket I'd been rummaging through. Once the doctor finished all the same steps the young lady had already done earlier, she looked up at me. "Okay, Libby. I don't see any issue here. Her vitals—all appear to be healthy. I find nothing of concern. Of course, we can run blood tests, just to be certain."

At this point, I was sure they were on to our charade and I only wanted out of there. I'd accomplished what we had come there for.

"Well, if all her vitals are good … I mean, I don't want to put her under any further undue stress. I'll just take her home and continue to monitor her."

"Very well," Dr. Fanter gave the tech a few instructions, said her goodbyes to Shadow and I, and walked out of the room.

As soon as I heard the hydraulic mechanism lowering the table, I began a more earnest look around for my phone.

"Lose something?" the lady asked.

I startled, not realizing she was watching me. "I'm not sure where I set my phone."

She handed Shadow's leash back to me and gave a cursory glance around the countertop. She made a few notes, then stated, "I need to make a copy of this—I'll be right back. Maybe you left your phone in the lobby?" She disappeared through the doorway and I got down on the laminate wooden floor.

There was a counter and cabinet combination, a shelving unit, the examination table, and the chair I had sat in. It's not as though there were many places for my phone to hide. That's when I saw a small space under the bottom shelf. *Oh crap!*

Just as I tried pulling it away from the wall, the technician walked back into the room.

"What are you doing?"

"Oh, sorry! I think my phone may have slid underneath this shelf."

"How?"

I took that as a rhetorical question and didn't bother answering, but I may or may not have cast a look toward Shadow, implicating her.

The technician didn't hesitate; she helped me slide the furniture over and there was my phone. So relieved, I shoved it into my pocket, grabbed the paperwork she handed to me, and led Shadow out the door into the lobby where we paid and promptly left the building.

Sitting in the car, I pulled my phone out and reviewed the photos. Relieved, I had a name and address for one of the poisoned dog's owners. I'd try to make contact after I was done with my clients' appointments late this afternoon.

CHAPTER FIFTEEN

As I worked on my last massage client of the day, my mind raced. Something about the conversation I overheard at the vet's office bothered me. *Why would they be concerned about my asking questions related to recent poisonings?* Especially when I was there under the guise of concern over my pup. Something about that hadn't set well with me. *Were they hiding something? What exactly were they afraid of?*

My attention shot back to the client on my table. He was a man who was slightly younger than me; I guessed he was in his mid-thirties. He'd asked me something when my mind was elsewhere. I hated when that happened.

"I'm sorry. What was that?" I asked politely.

His muffled voice started again. "Oh, I just mentioned my friend and I really enjoyed the shoulder massages we received at the festival. I'm so glad I booked this appointment. I'm going to make sure she gets in soon as well. What do you call this barefoot massage again?"

"Ashiatsu. Thank you for the recommendation as well."

"I think she was nervous that it meant that you'd walk on her back. But this is great ... and not scary at all."

"Oh no, I'd never walk on your back. But, yes, you are right ... we can work deeper into the tissues this way and it's less painful."

"So, how are you enjoying the festival?" he asked, changing subjects.

"It's a lot of work—but if we gain some new clients, like yourself, then it's definitely worth it."

"I've overheard some vendors—sounds like they've already pulled out from joining the festival next year. They don't like how it's being run."

"Oh, really?" That surprised me. I hadn't realized other vendors had already made those decisions. I understood how many were uneasy—we definitely were.

"Yeah, and vendors selling food products that are making people and animals ill. That's a shame. I won't be back. But I'm sure glad I found Dharma Inspired by being there this year!"

"Thank you—I'm happy you've found us, too."

He settled back into the massage and was quiet for the rest of the session. I hadn't realized how much of the general public knew about what was happening behind the scenes at the festival. That wasn't good—if rumors like that were getting out, everyone would lose customers.

Half an hour later, after seeing the client out, and encouraging his friend to schedule next time, too, I hurried back into the room to clean up. Shadow ran after me, which

I took as a sign that she'd been waiting around a little too long now.

One quick pull and the fitted sheet was off. Something flittered onto the floor. I bent down and found a folded piece of paper—a note. Carefully opening it, I read: **You're barking up the wrong tree.** My heart pumped. I jumped up and ran back through the spa to the front desk. Shadow barked and chased after me, obviously thinking we were playing a game.

"Oh jeez, Libby! You startled me!" Bella exclaimed. "What's wrong?"

"Did that man leave?" I opened the front door, peering out into the nearly empty parking lot.

"You mean your last client?"

I held up the piece of paper. "He left a threatening note."

"What?" She held out her hand and snatched the paper from me. "And he was so nice." She read the note. "What does this mean?"

"I don't know. But during his session, he mentioned the festival. You know, the crime and all. He knows what's going on there—and now *this*." I pointed at the note she still held. "It appears he is on to me."

"What do you mean, Libby?"

"He knows I've been asking questions. Maybe he knows I've been talking to the police? Maybe he's the one who *set me up*! I don't know."

"*Barking* up the wrong tree…" she re-read. "Could that be about Pupcakes? Has to be an intended pun, doesn't it?"

Shadow pawed at my leg and let out a low woof.

"Wait, what was his name again? Pull up the account on the computer," I instructed, and Bella's fingers flew with keystrokes. "Robbie Listler is how he filled out the form."

"He introduced himself as Rob. I'm not sure I recognize that name—do you?"

"No, why would we recognize the name? He's a new client."

"And no one we've met through the festival—like vendors or officials?"

"Not that I know of."

I nodded and kept reading the note, waiting for something to jump out at me.

"What's his phone number? I'll call him. I'm not afraid to ask boldly why he left me this note. Simple as that."

Bella glanced nervously at me before scrolling through his account information. She pulled out a Post-it, wrote down a number, and handed it to me. "Are you sure?"

I nodded and then headed back to finish cleaning up the therapy room. Anger wasn't the right word for what I was feeling—no, but I felt irritated, for sure. *No one harasses me in my place of business. If he has something to tell me, he needs to be a man about it.* I thought back to the conversation he initiated during his session. That would have been the time to discuss an issue if he had one. *What was this passive-aggressive behavior all about? Was he trying to frighten me? Or was he trying to frighten us from the festival?* He had mentioned other vendors pulling out for the next year.

Shadow led the way, walking Bella and me out of the building. It was dark and our two cars were the only ones in the parking lot. Bella agreed to take Shadow home with her, as I had a date. Still on edge, I glanced around nervously before we quickly got in our cars and drove away.

My phone rang through my car's hands-free mechanism. I punched the button on the steering wheel to answer.

"Have you left yet?" Greg's voice boomed through the speaker.

"Yep, just pulling out now. We're still meeting at the steakhouse, right?"

"Yeah, still sound good? I'm just leaving my work and should be there in ten minutes or so."

"Perfect! I'll meet you there."

* * *

Before we'd ordered our meals, my phone was buzzing. I looked at the display and saw it was Mom.

"I'd better take this," I let Greg know, scooting out of our booth. Keeping my voice low as I exited the building, I answered, "Hi Mom."

"Oh, I hope I'm not interrupting."

"Nope. We're going to eat in a few minutes, so I can't talk long. Whatcha need?"

"Libby, Margie isn't feeling well and the other ladies are still busy knitting more goods. I don't think I can keep the booth open all day long myself."

"You need help. Okay. Well, let's see what Jordan's doing tomorrow. I'm working the late shift, but have a massage session scheduled for morning."

"Jordan is shuttling kids around to their schools and then activities after school," she interjected.

"Shoot. Okay, let me think about it and see who I can…"

"Libby, another call is coming in. Let's talk later." She hung up, and I walked back inside just in time to place my order.

Soon Greg and I fell into a comfortable conversation

over an enjoyable meal.

"So the first day went well. Were you able to meet all your coworkers?" I asked.

"There are only a couple of people working in the office. It's strangely quiet there."

"What exactly do you do?"

"Mainly, I sell Tonto National Forest recreational passes. Looks like this facility is also where people bring their watercraft to get inspected and registered, so I'm sure I'll be doing that." The look on his face said he was less than thrilled.

"Bet you'd rather be outside in the forest?"

"Well, yeah, of course. But this is only temporary. I'm willing to help out where I'm needed. Oh! And I met an interesting guy today. He's here from the Alaska division helping on a search and rescue team up in the Superstitions. He had a black Labrador with him, so that's what sparked the conversation. That got me wondering if you've ever considered Shadow for search and rescue training? That's what this guy does—has a world-class training camp up there in Alaska, from the sounds of it."

"Sure, it's crossed my mind. She's brilliant at finding things, isn't she?"

"I think so."

"Hmm. Interesting, but I think I'm good keeping her solely as a pet—search and rescue, that could really change our lives. I mean, it involves the owners as much as the canine, right?"

He nodded while chewing his steak.

"Yeah, I'm not sure. Might look into it though. Never hurts to learn more about it."

He took a swig of his beer. "The one thing he said was,

'the younger, the better.' Anyway, how'd it go out at the fair today?"

I recapped the entire day, including the sleuth work that Shadow and I did at the veterinarian's office, as well as the strange note left by the new client. That reminded me I still needed to call both of the numbers that I'd tucked away in my purse. I hoped the dog owner would share the test results with me, since obviously the doctor's office wouldn't. And I needed the new client to explain that note he left for me. One thing was for certain: learning about the creepy message didn't thrill Greg too much.

* * *

Once we settled back in at home, I pulled out my laptop to check the next day's schedule. I'd had the thought that maybe we could lend a Dharma employee to help at Stitches of Love the next day. It looked like Bella had the day off. Everyone else had their schedules fully booked.

"You still working?" Greg asked, moving in beside me on the couch and gently nuzzling my neck.

"Not long, I promise. Especially if you keep that up," I mumbled, turning my head long enough for a kiss. "Just a few minutes, then I'm all yours."

He grabbed the remote control and scrolled through the TV menu. I sent Bella a quick text message asking if she'd be interested in helping my mom the next day. Then I got up to take Shadow out into the backyard and dialed the dog owner's number from the vet's paperwork photo I'd snagged.

The phone rang at least six times. No voicemail. No one answered. I hung up and tried again—I could have misdialed. As I watched Shadow sniff all over the backyard, I listened to the phone ringing endlessly. My mind wandered to our earlier conversation. *She could be a search and rescue dog—she'd be great.* I gave up and dialed the number Bella gave me for the client. It also rang and rang, with no voicemail set up. Frustrated, I put my phone back in my jeans pocket.

"C'mon, girl ... let's get back inside." She ran one more lap around the yard and then bounded through the open door.

Bella's text response came through within minutes and I called mom back, assuring her she'd have help. At least that was resolved, and now I could sit down and enjoy a movie with my man.

Greg enjoyed the action-adventure film, while I sat there attentively, but couldn't tell you one thing about the plot. Instead, my mind mulled over the conversation during the massage session. What I found odd about that was how I hadn't picked up on any strange vibes from the man. I'm usually quite adept at noticing these things. Then I thought, *what if he wasn't the one who wrote the note?* That was even more difficult for me to consider. I had cleaned the room, sheeted the massage table, and to my knowledge, no one else had gone in there. *Or had someone been in there?*

Why do new theories only surface close to bedtime?

CHAPTER SIXTEEN

Feeling as though I'd barely slept all night, I walked into the spa the next morning, and had barely set my purse down on my desk when Bella's call came in.

"Bella, what's up?" I answered.

"Libby, there's a news crew here asking questions. Your mom is on her way, but I don't feel comfortable talking to them. What should I do?"

"Can you see if Shelly or Yvette are in their booth?"

"Shelly's the one who called the media to begin with."

"What? Why?"

"I really don't know," she sighed loudly. "Oh wait, there's Julia now. Never mind. She'll handle this."

After hanging up with Bella, I dialed Shelly's number. Sure enough, she was aware of the press being at the festival. Apparently, she thought it would help donations for the hospital if the media knew about the theft at Stitches of Love. Although the sentiment behind it was well-meaning, I expressed that I really wished she had told one of us. I would have liked to be there for my mom, and with them being short-handed today, it wasn't the best of timing. Shelly said she'd head over there and see if she could assist. I wasn't sure that was exactly the solution we needed, but prayed she wouldn't make things worse. There was nothing I could do about it at this moment.

Quickly, I glanced at my watch—fifteen minutes until my session. I grabbed my lunch bag and headed to the breakroom. Putting the lunch in the fridge, I pushed the buttons on the Keurig and waited for my coffee. That's when my eyes caught sight of what was showing on the TV.

My mom!

I quickly grabbed the remote control and unmuted the sound. Sure enough, it was live footage during the channel's morning show. The reporter was standing in the street with a perfect shot of the Stitches of Love booth in the background. Standing at her side were Mom and Shelly.

"Here we are with … Julia Madsen, and…" she pointed her microphone to Shelly, who introduced herself. "Now, Julia, can you please tell us what the Stitches of Love charity does? What are you selling here?" The reporter and camera began walking closer to the booth. Next, I saw my mom pick up a small pink crocheted bunny. She hesitated for a second, but then the full personality of Julia Madsen came out and she explained all about her knitting club and the charitable work they do for the hospital.

The reporter's face became sullen as the cameraman zeroed back in on her. "And that's exactly what's so sad about *this year's* festival. We simply couldn't believe it, but thieves took advantage of Stitches of Love and this lovely lady, and they stole *hundreds* of their handmade goods." She turned back toward my mom. "And what does that mean for the charitable donations for the hospital?"

"Well, it means we won't be able to donate as much as we'd planned. It's terribly sad."

Shelly butted in. "If I may add?" she asked the reporter, holding up a large tin can which was decorated with Stitches of Love written across the front. "People can still donate to The Children's Hospital. Please. We encourage everyone to stop by this booth," she pointed to their signage, "and donate what you can. It's not the children's fault people do bad things—let's make up for what these horrible thieves stole from them. And, whatever is donated in *this can* here at the festival," she held it up to the camera, "Pupcakes & More will match the donation."

The reporter turned to question Shelly about Pupcakes & More, promising they'd broadcast from there during their next segment. Once it went back to the studio, I muted the TV again and grabbed my cup of coffee. My thoughts were swirling around as I walked back to my office. It had been good footage and a nice call-to-action for donations. That wasn't what bothered me. *So, why was I upset about the TV coverage?*

Sydney's voice broke through my concentration, and I looked up to see her standing in the doorway. My client was here, she let me know. Time to get to work.

By noontime, Sydney and I both headed to downtown Mesa. We opted to not share a ride since we both had commitments afterward.

From the moment we arrived, and after Lexi and Diane

left, we stayed in constant motion the entire afternoon. For the middle of a work week, it was plenty busy. Several times, I looked over at Pupcakes and noticed very little traffic compared to the rest of the vendors. Clearly, having been closed down for a few days hadn't helped their business. Wondering if the word had gotten out, I then remembered the client I had yesterday that made mention. That was my answer.

Once business slowed at the end of the day, Yvette wandered over.

"Wow, you guys have been slammed all day," she mentioned.

"I'm surprised as well—middle of the week and all." I gathered a pile of towels and shoved them into a laundry bag.

She looked put out, so I asked, "What's wrong? It's good that you're reopened, right?"

"Yes. Of course. I only wish Shelly hadn't talked to the media, though."

"Oh. You weren't part of that decision?"

"No. She sprung it on me, too."

"Well, it's good marketing … and we really appreciate the matched donations announcement." I hadn't talked to my mom yet, but felt sure she'd be thrilled about their generosity.

"That's what they say … even negative press."

"Negative?" I realized then that I hadn't seen their segment.

"Oh, the reporter was all over the dog poisoning part of the story. *Totally* backfired on Shelly. On us."

"Oh jeez. Sorry, I didn't realize."

"Yeah, I wish she had talked that over with me first. I

would have advised that we lie low for a while longer. At least until we know more."

"That reminds me. I got contact information about one of the dog owners. Haven't been able to reach them yet, but hoping to learn something soon."

"Cool. Hopefully, you find out before it blows up in our face … and over more news channels." Her half-hearted smile made me sad. These poor ladies.

Before I could tell her I had another appointment at the next veterinarian's office, the reporter walked up to our booth. No camera crew, but I noticed Sydney shied away and headed to the back of the booth. Yvette quickly said goodbye, asking me to call her later. I stepped up to the reporter I'd seen on the TV earlier that morning.

"Libby Madsen?" she asked.

"Yep, that's me."

"Hi, I'm Rachel Noone with Channel 6 News." She held out her hand and I shook it. "You're related to Julia Madsen?"

"Uh-huh. That's my mom."

"Libby, we understand you are a suspect in the theft case."

I stopped her right there. "No. That's not accurate…"

She rifled through her notebook. "You were questioned by the police…"

Feeling suddenly defensive, I blurted out, "Yes, I was. But I'm not responsible for theft."

"Look, we're investigating the festival's security breaches and crimes. We understand you are, too."

My eyebrows lifted. *What did they know?*

"Libby, I think we could help each other."

Not sure whether I trusted the direction this

conversation was headed, I asked her for her business card and informed her I would call her if I found anything worth reporting. There was something unsettling about the exchange. *Why ask me to work with her? Shelly called her in the first place—why not involve her instead? What did she mean they understood I was investigating?*

In order to avoid talking to the reporter, Sydney had nearly everything packed into our container by the time I was done. As soon as she left, I headed down the street to my mom's booth. Bella was busy loading their container, and I found my mom talking to a lady at the side of their tent. She introduced me to her as one of the knitting group ladies. She'd just dropped off several more blankets and a few stuffed animals.

"Did Sydney already leave?" the lady asked me.

I was caught off guard, unaware she knew my employee. "Uh, yeah, she just left for her car."

"Darn it, I was hoping she'd take some things I've got in my trunk. Oh well, I'll stop by her house later."

"You know Sydney?"

"Oh, sure ... should have started with that, I guess. She's my granddaughter!" the proud grandmother exclaimed.

"Oh! Well, then I'm very happy to meet Sydney's grandmother."

I could see that revelation equally surprised my mom. It really was a small world.

"I was so happy when she got hired at Dharma. That girl really needed to find a job. Needs a new, more mature crowd to hang with. Can't always rely on the boyfriend, if you know what I mean." She chuckled, then said her goodbyes.

Bella, Mom, and I got caught up on the morning's

events. It did not thrill Bella with all the news cameras being around earlier in the morning. My mom relished it and appreciated the donations. She showed the large tin can; it was completely full of money. It had to be a couple hundred dollars. I thought about what Yvette said and wondered if Pupcakes could *actually* match the donations. Surely, they could cover one day's worth of donations, but there were still four days to go. With all their potential legal trouble ahead too, I prayed Shelly hadn't overstepped without consulting with Yvette.

I'd forgotten I still needed to get home and grab Shadow and then visit another Tempe veterinarian this evening. With a peek at my watch, I saw I had exactly one hour to accomplish that—I'd better hurry, I explained, saying goodbye to Mom and thanking Bella again for coming through in a pinch. Then I hustled off.

* * *

I struck out again at the second veterinarian's office. These professionals value patient privacy, I've learned. Shadow sure earned her share of cookies, taking one for the team by pretending to be a sick patient.

By the time I settled into my place on the sofa after dinner, I felt defeated. How hard could it be to reach people these days? In human history, we have the most communication means, yet it's impossible to get someone to answer a darn phone call.

"Is there another way around?" Greg asked, waiting patiently for the bag of popcorn in the microwave.

"Hmm? What do you mean?"

"If you couldn't get anyone to talk at the vet's office,

maybe there's another way?"

I simply shrugged my shoulders. That's all I'd thought about since my appointment. We can't go traipsing back in there—they'd recognize both Shadow and me. *How else do I learn about the other dog owners?*

I smelled the buttery deliciousness coming from the kitchen. Greg and I enjoyed our movie while eating popcorn. I had to believe tomorrow would bring better results. Somehow. Some way.

CHAPTER SEVENTEEN

I awoke, startled. My dreams had been vivid. My heart was still racing.

The reporter. Maybe I share what I know and *she* can go ask the questions? I lay there thinking about it for a while, as Greg snored away next to me. Was I sure I wanted to get Rachel nosing around more? What unintended consequences would that cause? Would it make life even more difficult for the Pupcakes owners? Or maybe it would help them? I was so conflicted.

I crawled quietly out of bed. Shadow was eager to start her day, so I opened the back sliding glass door and let her out while I made a latte. When I joined her outside, she wanted to play fetch. I realized then how much this festival had disrupted our normal routine. By now, we would have gone for our morning run before coffee, as I generally try not to book massage sessions before ten. Instead, this week, the schedule was completely flip-flopped and different every morning. Thankfully, I could have Shadow with me each day, so she wasn't always cooped up at home. Still, I felt the need to get back to our normal routine.

For now, I had to shower and be out of the house within the next half hour to open up our booth. At the first break I could get, I'd call the reporter and see what we could work out.

* * *

Mom and Margie had crowds at their business all morning. I noticed most looked like Arizona's winter visitors, or snowbirds, as the locals called them. When I got a break, Shadow and I wandered over and saw their shelves full of goods.

"Wow! Your knitting ladies have been busy!" I said in awe.

Margie turned, looking at the overflowing shelves. Her face glowed as she explained, "Oh, our small group could have never accomplished this much this quickly. No, these are donations from the community! Can you believe it?"

"You're kidding me!" I noticed the tin can had grown in size now as well. It was now a used large coffee can, filled to the rim, and all before ten in the morning. "This is incredible."

"It's all because of that news report. Every knitting group in the valley, I think, has reached out and contributed in some way. Oh, and get this—your mom's friend Kathy with Just Ducky set up a Go, uh, something-or-another. Anyway, a money account for charity."

"Go Fund Me?" I asked.

"Yes! That's it. She's sharing our story on social media and it's gone … what do they say? … *viral?* Anyway, we've raised *thousands* now," she whispered the last part. "Oh, I gotta get back to helping your mother. Everyone wants to buy something!" She hurried off, waving as she went.

I turned, walking away, smiling at how cute the two of them were—they were definitely in their element. Remembering Shelly's plea to the community and the offer to match donations, I cringed again, wondering how they would manage and hoping it wouldn't make Yvette more upset.

I made a mental note to call my sister later—Mom and Margie would need help over the weekend and the twins were eager. That had me pulling out my phone to call the reporter now, before I got busy again. We agreed to meet at her offices after my festival shift and before my late afternoon massage appointments.

When I walked up to the booth, Shelly was signaling me over to theirs.

"Hey, Libby!" she hollered as I walked up. She was sitting on a high stool, no crowds in front of their booth. "Looks like they're doing great over there," she mentioned, pointing to the crowd. "I guess I really screwed up bringing in the media. I mean, it was great for your mom, don't get me wrong. But Yvette is livid with me now. That damn reporter won't stop snooping into our business and ever since her news report, business has sucked."

Having just hung up from a call with the reporter, I felt a twinge of guilt creep along my spine. *Should I have agreed to work with Rachel?*

"Hey, maybe it will work out in your favor, too?"

Focusing on the positive, I tried to deflect Shelly's vitriol. "Your company will be exonerated if there's nothing wrong with the product manufacturing," I said.

"In the meantime, people are afraid."

"True. I'm sorry about that. I hope we can get to the bottom of it before much more damage is done."

"Many businesses fail for reputational harm alone. This could absolutely ruin us."

"Well, I'm still nosing around. Unfortunately, I haven't been able to talk to the dog owners yet. Have one name so far, but haven't reached them yet. I've been to two veterinarian offices. Unfortunately, they are living by privacy rules and won't discuss anything with me. But, don't worry, we'll get there. I know people—we'll figure it all out, Shelly."

The corners of her mouth lifted slightly. "Thanks, Libby. I appreciate your help. Anything you can do about a mad spouse?"

I grimaced. "Uh, I'm not cut out for that type of work. But I'm sure things will settle down; give her time."

My phone rang, and I said goodbye to Shelly.

It was Chris, my lawyer. The officials had been collecting more camera footage throughout the week and had now shared more with him. He wanted to find a time today for me to view it.

"I think you'll find this very interesting," he said. "This could change everything."

I looked at my watch. I had another hour here before my shift was over. Two hours before meeting with the reporter, in downtown Phoenix. And four hours before my afternoon session began. How was I possibly going to manage all the appointments and driving time?

"I've got a heavy schedule today, but let me see what I can arrange. I'll text you in a bit to confirm the time."

As soon as we hung up, I got on the phone with the spa. Lexi was ready and could head to the booth a little early. Then I talked to Diane and asked if she'd be able to cover my massage session at four, if I got stuck downtown. Thankfully, she was available.

Quick text to Chris—I'll meet you outside the courthouse at noon.

Before I headed back inside, I caught some movement from the corner of my eye. Someone lurked around the side of our container. I sidestepped around the back corner of the booth only to see black boots retreating. Shadow barked and pulled me. We ran past the container, followed the walkway along the booth behind our row, and out into the street. A lady pushing a stroller nearly ran into us. Dodging her, I pulled Shadow to an opening in the crowd, tiptoeing and trying to look over everyone's heads. Since I couldn't see feet well, I had no idea which body wore the boots I saw. There wasn't anyone running; no one acting suspicious. We'd lost him, so we went back to work and waited for Lexi to arrive.

* * *

Later at the courthouse, my attorney turned on the TV. This was feeling like a routine now—sitting in cold, sterile rooms. I leaned in as the footage began.

"That's Zen Zone, right?" I asked. "I'm guessing that could be Jessica." It was dark and grainy, but the person loading the secure container appeared to be her size.

"Notice anything else?" Chris asked.

I shook my head. He let the segment play out and then restarted it. I watched carefully and then stared at Chris. "What am I missing?"

"You don't think this person could be mistaken for you? See here—similar clothing you both wear. What do they call it—athletic wear?"

Thinking there was a dig in there about my attire, I brushed it off. I squinted again at the dark figure on the screen. Was it Jessica? Since she was an owner of that business, that would make the most sense. Why do the police automatically suspect me? Mostly, I was struggling to remember earlier in the week when I had last seen Jessica. *Were we the same height?* We were both slender and athletic. I supposed we could be mistaken for one another. Maybe.

"I guess I could see that. I'm not sure she's really my height though? Is this the big 'game- changer' you mentioned?"

"Well, stick with me here. Let's look at a couple of others." Using his mouse, he fumbled around before finding the exact file he wanted to run next.

We watched closely. A gasp escaped me when I realized what Chris was onto. Sydney was loading our container— it looked like this was footage from the evening before. The dusk lighting cast deep shadows around our booth, particularly in the corner near the container. The first thing I noticed was that Sydney and Jessica looked oddly similar— clothing, physique, and the same ponytail—and doing identical tasks on video. Since the video wasn't in color, I could only tell the person's hair was darker, as opposed to having blonde hair. Specific color was impossible to make out. That wasn't what caught my breath, though.

"Can you replay, please?" I asked him.

This time, I kept my eyes glued to the surroundings and not the person loading their container.

"Yep, right there!" I yelled out. "Stop!" Of course, it was too late, and he had to replay it again.

"There!" I pointed to the deep shadows between the container and booth. "Someone is standing there. Now, press play again."

We watched as a dark form emerged from the shadows. What appeared was a barely perceptible illusion, following Sydney without her knowledge. The figure, taller than the young woman, dressed head to toe in all black, vanished equally undetected. Shadow let out a woof.

"What the ….?" I muttered, my hand slapping over my mouth.

Chris' eyes were wide. "Okay, so I never saw *that* earlier." He backed the footage up and slowed it way down. We watched again as an eerily ghost-like apparition slunk along the perimeter of our booth.

I shook off the chills before turning to Chris. "If this wasn't what was 'game-changing' then what was? Is there more?"

His eyes were fixated on the screen, continuing to slow the replay. "Uh, wow. This clearly adds another element. But, what I called you here today for … well, I concluded that there was *no way* to tell a difference between you, the lady at Zen Zone, and your worker. Libby, it's a game-changer because the prosecution does not have a case against *you*."

"Of course, they don't! I didn't do it!" I laughed. "But, Chris," I paused, pointing back to the screen. "*These* boots right here…" I got up and pointed at the grainy, dark image of the person's feet. "This person was lurking around our booth *this morning*! Right before I came here, in fact. It *has* to be the same person. I've seen these boots! Someone is stalking us."

A low growl came from Shadow, still sitting next to my chair.

Chris sat there quietly for a moment. "Why would someone stalk you?"

"Maybe they don't like me snooping around?"

His face squinched up, not pleased with my answer. "Are you snooping around, Libby?"

I gave one shoulder a slight shrug. "Maybe."

He used the remote to turn off the TV. Then unhooked his computer and gathered his paperwork into the rolling case. "Libby, I need you to leave the thefts to the authorities. They'll find the culprit. I'm going to keep you out of jail— but if you go sticking your nose where it doesn't belong, I can't promise I'll be successful. So, *please*, leave it alone."

I stood and watched him open the door. I didn't agree or disagree with his plan. However, anyone who knows me well understands I *can't* leave this alone. I *will* find out who is responsible.

CHAPTER EIGHTEEN

During my forty-minute journey to the Channel 6 offices, I kept hearing my attorney's warning. Knowing he was only doing his job, I wasn't upset and I'm sure he meant well. However, I don't trust the police to get the job done on their own. At least, not in a timely fashion without me sitting in a jail cell first. I've seen it before, where they latch onto the first suspect and then build their entire case around that. Also, I wasn't convinced that the authorities had enough resources to dedicate much attention to the crimes happening in our city, let alone at the festival. They *needed* me.

I chuckled at that last thought as I pulled into the parking garage and grabbed my ticket from the dispenser. Winding my way up to the fifth level, I finally found a suitable spot in the visitor's parking. Before I got out of the car, my phone rang.

"Hey sweetie," I answered, remembering I hadn't even spoken to Greg all day. "How's your day at work?"

"Good. All is well. Will I see you tonight? Want me to pick up something from the store, maybe?"

"Oooh, that sounds great. Yes, please." I filled him in on my schedule and let him know I should be home around six if everything went to plan. I'd left Shadow at home, but Bella was going to be in and out throughout the afternoon, so I wasn't worried about her. He promised to take her for a walk when he got home. "Okay, I've got to run … have an appointment in ten minutes."

The elevator let me off in the Channel 6 lobby. Security guards stood inside each door and on either side of secure gates that led to another bank of elevators.

"Can I help you, ma'am?" one of them asked.

"I'm here to see Rachel Noone."

He picked up a phone and announced my arrival.

"Please, have a seat over there." He pointed to a grouping of chairs where one other person sat. "She'll be down in a moment."

I did as I was instructed, noticing the person already sitting was a fairly well-known anchor from a rival station. Smiling, I said a quick hello as I sat down, without gawking or giving away that I recognized him. *Were anchors famous people?* I thought to myself. I also wondered whether it was standard practice for rivaling newspeople to hang out with each other. *Are they acquaintances? Do they share information?* I'd always thought they competed with one another.

The elevator dinged, and I looked up to see the tall blonde reporter swipe her badge and walk through the security gates toward me. I noticed that the evening anchor couldn't keep his eyes off her.

"Hi Libby!" she exclaimed, without noticing the other man at all. "So glad you could make it. Come with me."

She was as bubbly as ever, chatting at a feverish rate as we made our way to the twentieth floor. I wondered if TV personalities ever had an off switch. I was also curious to know whether they got an allowance for clothing. They always wear the most fashionable clothes and style themselves perfectly. *Was it like a movie set and they provided stylists for them? Clothing on racks from which they could choose a new beautiful dress daily?* Of course, none of this was why I'd come here, but that's how my brain works most days.

We walked into a small conference room with six chairs around a rectangular table. Rachel offered me a bottle of water and I accepted.

"What made you call me back?" she asked.

"I wanted to set a few things straight," I answered matter-of-factly.

"Oh?"

"First, someone has targeted Pupcakes & More. They are not poisoning dogs! Please help get that information out there."

She pulled over a notepad and pencil from the center of the table, poised to write. "And what evidence do you have to support that claim?"

"They're my friends. Their love for animals—well, if you knew them, you'd know in an instance they don't harm dogs."

"That's not proof, Libby."

My pulse quickened. What was I thinking? Why had I come here? Suddenly I felt I'd stepped into the lion's den. Even more so than being questioned at the police station.

However, she was right. What proof did I have?

"You're right. And, to be fair, I haven't known them long." I took a swig of the water, feeling sweat form at my brow. "However, have you been in touch with the FDA?"

She shook her head.

"Ok. Contact Bart Littel with the FDA. They did a thorough inspection of the Pupcakes manufacturing plant and could not come up with one infraction that would shut it down. That's proof."

She wrote down the name. "Thanks, that helps. I'm not sure it proves they didn't provide dogs with tainted treats at the festival, though."

I thought about that for a second. "Doesn't it at least suggest that somehow the product was contaminated outside of their production plant? If manufacturing wasn't the cause, then something happened once it left there, right?"

"I see where you're going." She jotted down several more things. "Who has the best access to their product?"

"Well, of course, they do."

"And to be very clear, who are *they*?"

"The owners—Shelly and Yvette."

"Right. So there's the means and opportunity."

"But what would their motive be? *Why* would they want to sabotage their own business? That makes no sense whatsoever."

"And I agree with you. There's more to the story."

"There have been other crimes committed, too. We can't ignore the possibility that all these crimes could be related." As I made the statement, I contemplated how much I should divulge to Rachel. *Should I tell her about the video footage? How much had she already figured out?*

"Yes, and about those … your mom's product was recovered. The Zen Zone bath products were found," she hesitated, clearing her throat, "in, er, *your* booth."

She had delved into this more. Rachel stood up and begin pacing the length of the table.

"Libby, what do you think I can do for you?" she asked.

I couldn't come up with words and stared at her questioningly.

"Well, you called me. Why?" she prompted.

"Uh, I guess because I want to clear my name. I'm a suspect in theft at Zen Zone and I'd like to avoid arrest. Also, I'm not convinced the police are doing enough."

Still walking around the room anxiously, she asked, "Then why has our entire conversation today been about Pupcakes & More?"

"Because that crime is the most serious. I mean, as you stated, the bath bombs and knitted goods have already been recovered. But if dogs actually were harmed, we *have* to find out who did it. What if it happens again? We can't risk more innocent animals becoming ill! I'm convinced everything's related—and for some reason, we're being set up. I don't know the why, how, and who."

She halted and turned back to me. "Wait, wait. You said, 'actually harmed'. Do you believe the dog owners are lying?"

"That's it! That's precisely what you could do to help me!"

"What?"

"Help me find the victims—well, the dog owners. I'm not calling them liars, but how do we know the organic treats were responsible for making the dogs ill? I don't even know how many dogs in total have been harmed.

What if that's been exaggerated?" I explained how I'd tried snooping around at the vet's offices with little luck. "Maybe as a reporter, you have better luck? More resources?"

"In my experience, people see a reporter coming and they run," she chuckled. "Like your worker the other day. Doesn't matter. Investigative reporting is my job and I will deal with slammed doors and being hung up on. Let's figure out who's behind this, Libby." She smiled, and she sat back down next to me. "I have to warn you, though. I am going to report the facts—no matter who gets implicated. You may not like that."

The butterflies fluttered in my gut. "Yes, I understand. I'm confident we'll get the bad guys." I sure hoped I was right.

We wrapped up our conversation with me sharing the names and phone numbers I had. I also divulged what I'd seen on the video. She admitted they continued to wait for officials to turn over camera footage and appreciated what I'd divulged. She still wanted to see it and I promised I'd ask Chris if he could arrange that. Since he had scolded me earlier, I dreaded having the conversation, and only hoped that the news station would come through for her soonest.

Driving back across the valley, I felt hopeful that the added efforts would assist in justice for my new friends. At the very least, I prayed I hadn't just made the worst decision of my life.

CHAPTER NINETEEN

Bella and Sydney were in my living room when I walked through the door. Greg and Shadow I could see through the glass door in the backyard. The aroma of food grilling wafted through the room, making me realize how many hours it'd been since I'd had any.

"Hey, ladies," I said as I set my bag on a barstool and walked through to the backdoor.

"I hope you don't mind, Libby," Sydney started. "Bella invited me over to do the new Pilates workout with her. Greg invited me to stay for dinner."

"The more, the merrier!" I stepped out onto the back patio and Shadow came bounding up to me. I took the ball from her mouth and threw it the distance of the small yard.

"Southern bourbon chicken. Sound good?" Greg asked, leaning over to give me a kiss. "Hope you're hungry. Look at these monstrous hunks of chicken, and I think Bella and Sydney whipped up a salad."

"I'll go pour a glass of wine," I said, picking up his nearly empty one. "Want a refresh?"

He nodded and I went inside, followed by my faithful pup. As soon as she saw Sydney, she started barking at her.

In the kitchen, Bella shouted, "Shadow! Stop that!" Then to me, "She keeps barking at Sydney. We've been through the introductions like a hundred times, and she's given her a cookie and everything."

I stooped over to pet Shadow and quiet her. "Hey, hey, hey. Shadow, Sydney is our friend. It's okay." There was one low growl, and then she laid down as I instructed. I stood up and gave her the stay command.

"Sorry, Sydney. She doesn't do that at the spa, does she?"

She shook her head. "I think it's because you're usually with her when she sees me at the front desk. Maybe since you weren't here this afternoon?"

I poured the two glasses of wine and set them on the table. "Help yourselves to drinks, our master-griller says dinner's nearly ready."

Bella pulled a large salad bowl from the refrigerator and took it to the table before coming back and pulling some delicious smelling dinner rolls from the oven. Once Greg brought the meat to the table, we all took our seats and dug right in.

"So, how'd the rest of the afternoon go in the booth?" I asked Bella.

"Great! Lexi was busy with chair massage and we must have passed out thousands of brochures."

Sydney piped up, "I've booked *so many* appointments! I think every therapist is going to be busy for months."

"That's fantastic. I wish we could say the same for our neighbors."

All eyes looked at me questioningly.

"At Pupcakes & More," I took a sip of wine, "their business has dropped off to nothing. Shelly and Yvette are at each other's throats. It's not good."

Greg sighed. "That really sucks. No nicer ladies than those two."

I nodded in agreement, chewing and contemplating whether I'd mention my meeting with the reporter. Deciding to hold back on that, keeping it my little secret, I asked Greg about his day at the Forest Service offices. He told us all about the two boats he inspected, and the handful of recreational passes he sold. Other than that, he helped the administrator move some furniture around and reorganize the office. As positive as he tried to make office work sound, I saw it on his face. This arrangement would not be satisfying work for long. This ranger needed to be doing outdoor work. He wanted to save forests and people, not move desks.

Sydney got up to clear her plate from the table, and immediately Shadow was on edge. She watched the girl's every move.

"Okay, c'mon, Shadow," I grabbed her collar to pull her closer to me. "Sit. Down." Once she was lying down on the floor again, I gave the stay command. This behavior was new, but then again, she was just a pup. Even a one-year-old was still learning. And other than the Johnsons, we hadn't regularly had new people in the house. Maybe that was it. I needed to socialize her more in the home.

Not long after dinner, Sydney thanked us for the meal

and went home. She was working the early shift in the morning and already had a long day.

Greg cleared the rest of the dishes from the table and I joined him at the sink to help load the dishwasher. "She seems like a nice girl," he commented.

Bella was putting leftovers in containers. "I've sure enjoyed having someone closer to my age to work with."

"Yeah, she seems to be working out well," I added.

"You know, it wasn't only about Pilates that I asked her over this evening. I mean, we did that, but she's been a good sounding board lately. I've opened up to her about Mom."

I set down the cup in my hand and turned around. "Really?" Bella hadn't opened up to anyone but me and her therapist about her childhood trauma.

"Well, some parts, not everything." She put the containers into the refrigerator and began wiping down the countertops. "You know, Sydney's childhood wasn't easy either. She's also probably happy to have someone to share with."

Bella stopped short of elaborating on what had happened to Sydney, which was probably smart since I was her employer, and it wasn't my business.

"Have you decided on whether to visit your mom?" I cautiously inquired.

She shrugged, eyes cast downward. She muttered, "Still considering." Then she perked up and smiled. "But Sydney offered to drive me if I go ahead with it! So maybe I will."

I caught Greg's glance. He saw my eyes fill when I turned back to the sink. I never responded, but each of us finished our final touches on cleaning the kitchen. Bella went to her room, and Greg and I attempted to watch some TV. My concentration wasn't with the programming.

"That hurt, didn't it?" Greg finally whispered close to my ear.

I nodded. My eyes filled with tears again, this time spilling over. His arms wrapped around me and held me tight.

"I don't know why. She's a grown woman," I muttered into his chest. "And it's not like she's my daughter."

"Well, you've been here for her since we found her, and since Maggie's incarceration. Gave Bella a home. A job." He sighed, shaking his head. "I mean, Libby, I felt that sting for you. I get it."

The tears kept falling. It hurt. When I could speak again, I softly explained. "I know. I've done so much for her and thought *I* was her confidante."

Choking up again, I added, "Don't get me wrong, I'm so happy she's made friends ... she needs lots of support from many. What do they say? *It takes a village...*" I mimicked.

Greg chuckled.

"But, when it comes to Maggie, her *mother*, I just ..." Words escaped me. Tears crept down my cheeks onto his shirt as he pulled me in closer.

"It's okay, let it all out," he consoled.

There was no watching television tonight. The week had taken its toll, leaving me an emotional mess. Facing arrest, wanting to help Shelly and Yvette, and worrying about Mom and Margie, John and Jessica. Even though some goods had been recovered, I was hell-bent on discovering who was responsible. Right now, all I needed was a good night's sleep.

CHAPTER TWENTY

Pulling up into the parking space before daylight the following morning, my eyes took in the surrounding cars. I hadn't seen Sydney's little VW bug on my way in, but there were many garage levels. She could already be here. I texted her and waited for a second, sipping my coffee. No response.

"Okay, Shadow," I turned around to face the backseat, seeing my pup's head tilt left. "Shall we get going?" Her tail beat against the seat, and a small whimper escaped her.

I opened the door and slid from the seat, placing my phone in my jeans' pocket. My purse strap, I draped over my neck, moving my arm through so it rested securely across my body and freed up my hands. Shadow was raring to go by the time I got the back door open and grabbed her leash. Thinking of the person I'd caught lurking around, I attached my handy pepper spray can to the handle of the leash, just in case.

"Libby!" I twisted around to see where the voice came from. It was Sydney, several rows over. She quickly made her way over to us. "I got your text, but was driving. Anyway, we made it! Oh, look how excited Shadow is!" she cooed as she reached out to pet her.

She sure was perky for five o'clock in the morning. *I need far more coffee before I could reach her level of enthusiasm,* I thought. I also noticed Shadow winced when Sydney reached for her, but never barked. Maybe she had been territorial at the house last night after all.

We walked the several blocks and made our way to our booth, saying good morning to the vendors along the way. Everyone greeted Shadow, but I'm not even sure they looked up at her human. I've become accustomed to being secondary this way.

"Oh, let's stop here for a coffee. Do you want one?" I asked Sydney.

She shook her head. "Nah, I'll go on ahead and get things started."

Now that we were amongst the vendors and not in an isolated parking garage, it would probably be okay to split up. I nodded and turned to place my order as she went on. Shadow sat staring after her until she disappeared around the corner.

"Large almond milk latte please," I said to the man at the coffee stand. "Oh, and one of those scones as well." I reached into my purse and pulled out some cash as I waited.

Shadow stood and tugged at the leash. "What is it, girl?"

I glanced around and couldn't see anything she'd be interested in. A small line had formed for coffee, but other than that, it was still quiet out. She whined again. "We'll get going here shortly. You gotta be patient," I chuckled, as I pulled my phone and scrolled through the notifications. "Nothing but bad news in the world—a war going here, someone shot over there, and politicians arguing over everything. We gotta stop reading this stuff, huh?" I said aloud to Shadow, but clearly her mind was on something else entirely.

I put my phone away and grabbed my coffee when my name was called, then tugged at the leash to get her going. "What is it, Shadow? Let's go…" I tried another gentle tug and finally she succumbed.

Just a few booths away from ours, a voice startled me. Yvette.

"Good morning," I said, trying hard not to appear as jumpy as I felt. Then I saw the look on her face. "Oh no, what's wrong?"

She paced in small circles, her hands communicating as loudly as her words. "We're going to lose it all, Libby! Everything we've worked so hard for!"

"Has something else happened? Do you have results from the toxicology tests?"

"No results yet. But the media is interviewing *everyone* in our orbit. I tell you, Shelly has really done it this time!"

I reached out and touched her shoulder. "They may actually be able to help," I softly added.

"Oh, not you, too!" she exclaimed.

"No. Wait, wait, wait," I called after her as she walked away. "I choose no sides. Don't worry."

She turned and waited for us to catch up.

"Please. Hear me out." I paused, considered updating her on how Rachel was going to help us, but after her reaction, I tried another tactic instead. "First, if there's nothing to hide, what's the worry?"

She let out a groan, tilting her face to the sky.

"I mean, really. What's the harm with the investigation if there's nothing to hide?"

"Libby, I don't want all my dirty laundry aired!"

"Okay. That's fair. Do you mind me asking about your 'dirty laundry'?"

I wasn't sure she was going to answer my question. We continued walking along, and now we approached our booths. Before I nearly gave up and headed off to work, she cleared her throat and pulled me away from Pupcakes.

"Um, well … you see, I may have a prior record. And, uh, I haven't exactly told my wife about it."

I nodded. That sounded like a good reason not to have a reporter nosing around.

"Don't tell me you've poisoned live beings in the past?" I giggled nervously.

She cracked a tiny smile. "No."

"Business fraud?"

"No."

"Anything related to what is going on here?"

"No."

"Then I don't think you have anything to worry about." I shrugged it off, then hesitated. "But it's not the business you're truly worried about, is it?"

"No."

"You're more worried about Shelly finding out your secret."

"Yes."

"Okay. Well, I don't need to know any more than that. My advice—friend to friend—is to level with her. Get it out in the open. This stress will do you damage the longer you hold on to it. Honesty is always the best policy."

She didn't exactly look happy, but when she saw Shelly, she hugged me and whispered, "Thanks for listening, Libby."

When Shadow and I walked into the tent, Sydney already had everything set up and was preparing more tri-fold brochures to hand out in the crowd. Shadow gave a low growl, but let Sydney pet her again and then she took her place on the doggy bed, where she could see the street. The sun shone and we could see the first customers milling about.

"Everything okay over there?" Sydney asked, signaling next door to Pupcakes & More. "Yvette looked upset when you guys walked up."

"Ah, nothing new. Worried about their business."

She folded the paper in front of her in thirds and asked, "Are there any new leads?"

"Not that I know of," I answered. "What have you heard amongst the vendors? You've been getting out of the booth more than I have."

She looked startled by the question. "Uh, no. Nothing."

"And when the investigator came around ... did he have questions for you?"

Avoiding eye contact, Sydney stood, looking out front. "Hmmm. No. Haven't been questioned by anyone. But I don't know anything, so…"

A customer approached, and Sydney jumped right in to help answer questions about the spa. She pointed out the lotions and oils we sell; I realized what a good sales person she was, so perfectly employed at the front desk at our spa. She enchanted the customer, who listened to her every word.

Something from our conversation hadn't settled well for me, I realized, standing there watching her. Remembering back to the meeting I had with my attorney and the video we watched, and seeing Sydney in the footage. They had questioned the rest of us. Over the past several days, everyone had approached us, whether it was the police, reporters, or the FDA investigator. Why didn't anyone question Sydney? Seemed odd.

Another customer walked up, and before I knew it, the morning turned to noon.

* * *

Rachel phoned me while I was out scrounging up some good ol' fried fair food for the gang. Kathleen and Bella had arrived, and I volunteered to feed everyone before I headed out for the day.

"Libby, I've spoken to one of the dog owners. The lady with the spaniel."

"Was she willing to talk?"

"Well, sort of … we got there in the end. Anyway, the tox screen should be back any day now. I could confirm the small dog—the cocker spaniel—had stomach upset for several days. She was lethargic, could hardly hold herself upright."

"Oh jeez. Did she say what made her think it had been the treats?"

"It was the only new thing the dog consumed."

"That she knows of. Dogs are always getting into

something," I added.

"Yeah, I guess. Anyway, she seemed willing to share whatever she learns from the reports when they come back. You know, as a concerned fellow dog owner."

"Ah, that's how you did it! Wonder why she wouldn't answer my calls?"

"Can't say, but I don't know she would have answered mine, either. I went to her neighborhood and waited until I saw them out on a walk."

Recognizing that as a tactic I used myself, I stood a little taller. "Oh, okay. So, the dog is doing better now?"

"Oh yeah, the vet flushed her with IV fluids for a couple days and she's on a bland diet since. Whatever was in the system is out now."

"That's good to know. Okay, well, it'll be interesting to know what the other dog owner has to say. Have you found them yet?"

"Not yet. Still working on it, though. But, Libby, there is one other thing   "

My pulse quickened. "What's that?"

"I've learned of at least five other dogs who've become ill. It wasn't only these two names you gave me from the FDA's initial report."

"Oh, crap."

We hung up, and I wasn't sure I had the heart to tell Shelly and Yvette what Rachel shared. I'd actually done well staying away from both of them since the morning conversation, so I decided then to keep that up. It's hard enough managing a relationship of one's own. I genuinely felt I needed to stay out of theirs. Still, my heart hurt for both of them. It's difficult for me, seeing others struggle.

With three large bags of various food items, I entered

our tent and cleared a space on the table in the back. Bella was helping a customer, but Kathleen and Sydney dug right into the bag, finding their orders. I found my cheeseburger and sat down on a folding chair.

Kathleen filled us in on business back in Mesa. "Lexi has had her hands full this morning. I believe Bella said she booked another ten appointments for next week."

"All for Lexi?"

"No, between all of us, but all *new* clients. That's great, isn't it?"

"I was skeptical when Lexi signed us up for this. How wrong I was!" I laughed.

"How're your mom and Margie getting on down the way? I heard the news report really helped them," Kathleen inquired.

"That it did," I mumbled, with my napkin in front of my mouth, after taking a bite. I caught a drip of ketchup and finished chewing, then added, "I'm relieved. Day one of the festival, I thought for sure they were done." I detailed everything they'd updated me about, related to the local knitting groups and the online donations.

"Some are luckier than others, I suppose," Kathleen commented, as she crinkled up her food bag and tossed it into the trash bag. She pointed to her right. "They are not so lucky."

"Oh, I know!" I decided I'd leave it at that. I cleaned up my lunch and gathered my stuff. Shadow was helping Bella finish up her fries and didn't want to be pulled away, but we needed to go. We still had to run by my sister's house before getting back to the spa for an afternoon appointment. Sometime, I also needed to check in with Greg.

As I was walking out, I saw Sydney was still handing out fliers across the lane. That wasn't what startled me. It was *who* she was talking to that made me stop in my tracks.

CHAPTER TWENTY-ONE

By the time I set down the bags I'd already picked up and walked out of the booth, Sydney was on her way back and already talking with someone else. When she came closer, I asked who the lady was she'd been talking to.

"Uh, I'm not sure. A festival-goer? That's all I know."

"She came to inspect our spa a couple of weeks ago, and I'd like to talk to her. She didn't give you any contact information or anything?"

"Uh, nope. But maybe she'll call and schedule a massage—you could talk to her then."

"And you're sure you hadn't seen her before?"

She shook her head and walked into the booth.

* * *

Driving over to my sister's, my mind kept going back to when I saw Sydney with the woman. I swore their conversation looked as though they were familiar with one another. But what was it exactly that made me think that? I couldn't pinpoint it.

When my sister answered her door, Ryan, the toddler, hung tightly to her leg, only quickly peeking out at me. I went inside and tried to peel him away, to no avail. Even Shadow instigating play wasn't working today.

"What was it you wanted to see me about?" I asked.

"Well, Mom had told me all about the vendors whose products have made the dogs sick. She said something about you trying to find out more from the owners. I've met one lady in our mommy-and-me class!" She pointed her finger downward at Ryan. "She was saying how sick her dachshund had been ever since going to the festival."

"Really? I would love to talk to her." Then I had a horrifying thought. "That doesn't entail me going to mommy-and-me class, does it?"

She laughed, "No, Silly! I've got her number in here." She tried to turn and walk into the kitchen. "Ryan, mommy needs you to let go now," she said sweetly to the child. She pried his little fingers off and held them in her hand, urging him to walk with her.

Shadow and I followed them into the large kitchen and family room area. The TV showed animated little guys running around speaking gibberish. I'm sure it made sense to Ryan, but I wasn't following.

"Oh, here we go." She grabbed a towel and wiped off the paper. "Don't worry, just a little apple juice."

"Did she say whether she had been to the Pupcakes & More booth? Does she believe their treats caused her dog to be sick?"

"You know, it was kind of chaotic with the kids. I caught bits and pieces of what she was saying, but I'm really not sure about that. Since I knew from Mom about that booth next to your little business ... and she also mentioned you were helping the owners clear their name ... I thought this lady might be of help. Not sure if it's related or not, though. Give her a call. Really sweet girl. Young." Jordan explained then that she had school pickup duty and would have to get going. "Getting this one out the door takes *forever*." She rolled her eyes, pointing to her child, and grumbled, "I best get started now!"

I gave her a giant hug, and we promised to get together again soon. I tried again to kiss Ryan, but he quickly bolted to his room. Maybe next time.

* * *

Shadow and I worked hard the rest of the day at the spa. She helped Diane at the front desk and provided comfort to a couple of our clients in the Serenity Room. Her favorite thing about spa work was all the attention she received. Everyone loved having a fur-baby around. Plus, I suspected a few crumbs from the clients' treats found their way to the floor occasionally. She figured this out ages ago, and I'd see her place herself right at their feet.

Back in my office shortly after five, I tried the phone number Jordan had given me. Used to no one answering when I placed phone calls, I took a large swig of my water.

"Hello?" a high-pitched, sweet voice answered.

One large gulp and I attempted to respond, only I ended up breathing in some of the water. Choking now,

I tried again, "Hi." But all I could do was cough urgently.

"Hello?" she impatiently repeated.

"I'm sorry. One second." I tried swallowing a small sip between coughs.

"If you're selling anything, the answer is no!"

"Wait, wait. I promise I'm not selling anything." I got that much out with one more throat-clearing action, then added, "Please. My name is Libby Madsen. You know my sister."

"Oh? Who's your sister?"

"Jordan White—you both attend mommy-and-me classes."

"Right. Oh! She said something about her sister looking into the sick dog cases. Is that right?"

"Yes! Thank you!" I took another small sip of water. "Britney, I was wondering if you could share your story?"

"Umm, sure? Uh, I'm not sure what story I have to tell exactly."

"Maybe you could start with what you told the other mommies during class?" I prompted.

"So, we went to the festival last weekend in Mesa. Wow, they've really expanded from years back—I was impressed. So was Dolly."

"Dolly?"

"My dachshund. She's six now, little Dolly. My husband, Dolly, our two-year-old, Ethan—we spent an afternoon walking around. It was a lovely day."

I patiently listened, but found my hands frequently motioning to 'speed things up', even though she couldn't see me. All my effort was required to simply sit and listen. Glancing at the phone's display, I noticed my mother trying to reach me partway through the phone call. I let it go to voice mail; I'd have to call her back. The young mother wanted to share every detail of their day, from everything they bought, to what they ate, and how many times both their babies had 'to go'. Finally, we got to the part where they'd bought the organic treats and later that night, Dolly started vomiting. Overnight, it got even worse, taking the dog outside throughout the night. By morning, Dolly was lethargic. No energy at all. She joked how the two-year-old, Ethan, was the only one left with any energy which didn't do any of them any good.

"And what did the veterinarian say about the illness?" I asked, noticing another phone call coming through. This time from Lexi. I also let it go to voice mail.

"Oh, we never ended up taking her to the vet. I attempted to feed her a bland diet—you know, boiled chicken and white rice—she showed little interest in food that first day. By the second day, though, when I was going to call the vet, she perked right up. Ate the chicken and rice and has improved every day since. Something just didn't agree with her. We suspect it was the new treats we gave her. I mean, that can happen."

"Does she regularly have sensitivities to food?"

"Not generally. And, we only feed her organic. We thought the Pupcakes & More treats would be great. I mean, they sound amazing. I'd eat them!" She laughed. "But sometimes our tummies don't like new stuff."

"So, you never reported the illness to anyone—not even the support line at the dog food company?"

"Nah. I mean, things happen." She paused for a second. "However, I've seen the news reports now. Should I be concerned?"

"No, no. I don't think there's cause for alarm. I know

firsthand that the FDA inspected their manufacturing and hadn't found anything."

"But they still don't know what's causing the sickness in the dogs?" she asked.

"That's right."

"Hmmm. Maybe I should report it, then?"

I honestly wasn't sure what to advise. If it were my dog, I probably would. Since the owners were my friends, I felt a little protective. *But what if their product was harming canines in the community?* No one knew one-hundred percent what was causing the problems. I left it for her to make that decision, offering no advice. Before we hung up, I promised to let her know if we learned anything new and I thanked her for sharing her story.

As I put my phone back in my pocket, Lexi walked in the door. She looked beat.

"Long day, huh? Sorry I missed your call," I said, picking up my phone and scrolling through the notifications. "Uh, oh, *calls*," and then I noticed her expression; it wasn't only about exhaustion. "What's going …"

"Libby, your mom is in the hospital."

CHAPTER TWENTY-TWO

The whoosh of the automatic sliding glass doors immediately transported my mind back to the time when my mom and I rushed into the emergency room looking for my father. The antiseptic smells, patients' groans, and the pervasive look of sadness from everyone in the lobby—all of it came back. Only this time, we were there for my mother.

I rushed to the desk, asking for Julia Madsen, and was told to take a seat. The doctor would be out to speak to us soon. When I turned to find a seat, I saw John and Jessica, Shelly and Yvette, and Bella all walking toward me. They guided me to a corner of the room where we could be seated together for the long wait.

On the drive over, I learned from Lexi that mom had

collapsed. No one quite knew what caused it, but John found her unconscious on the ground at the side of their booth. Jessica called 9-1-1 and ran over to the Dharma booth to find me. When she learned I wasn't there, Lexi followed her back and began her attempts to get hold of me.

Everyone seated around me talked about the steps they took, but my clouded mind couldn't process any of it. I only wanted to know what happened to my mother. *Had it been a medical issue? Or was someone responsible for harming her?* I couldn't let my mind rummage through those alternatives. Closing my eyes, I tried to block everything around me. Then I remembered, and my eyes flew open.

"Lexi, where's Shadow?" I asked her in a panic.

"Greg got her from the spa to take her home. Don't worry, he'll be here soon."

I closed my eyes again. The voices jumbled all together. Some pieces of conversation I picked up, but mostly, the sounds echoed, bouncing around in the recesses of my mind. Then I clearly heard a male voice, "Family of Julia…" and I jumped up. Lexi stood with me, holding on at the elbow, steadying me.

A middle-aged man in blue scrubs covered by a white coat stepped forward and introduced himself as a neurologist. Dr. Havel. He asked about my relationship with Julia Madsen. Surprisingly, my brain engaged, and I answered all his questions with clarity, explaining I was her daughter. I listened intently, hearing only his voice and tuning out the other superfluous noises around me.

"Your mother has suffered from a small brain bleed." His voice was soft, but steady. "We believe this was from a blow to the head. She either hit her head and fell, or fell, hitting her head. We've had to relieve the pressure that built because of the bleeding, but she was fortunate she had received immediate help at the scene. Overall, her prognosis is good. She's responding well and we're hopeful for a complete recovery."

I let out an enormous sigh. "When can I see her?"

"Ms. Madsen, she's still unconscious and requires rest. In the coming days, we'll need to run a battery of tests to determine … uh, to determine functionality. Communication may be affected and it could take a while to get back."

"But you just said she responded well!" Tears welled, and I caught sight of Greg barreling into the lobby. He came up on the other side of me and listened intently as the doctor continued his explanation.

"Yes. Her vitals are responding well. The bleed wasn't extensive, only meaning that we've seen worse. However, it's still way too early to know how long her recovery will take. Everyone responds differently. I have every confidence she *will* recover—but these things take time."

Lexi hugged me. "It'll be okay, Libby." Then she turned to the doctor and asked, "Do you think she'll be able to see her tonight?"

He hesitated, then turned to me. "I'll let you see her for a couple of minutes. Only you—" he looked out at the rest of our friends who'd gathered, then warned me, "As I said, she needs rest, and I'm sure you'll have better visiting time with her in the coming days than you would tonight anyway. It might be best for you to go home and then be here tomorrow for her."

I wanted to see her, so I followed the doctor through the doors and down the hallway.

As we approached the room, I could see a multitude of

tubes and wires attached to her. White bandaging encased her head and I let out a gasp. I walked through the doorway and cautiously walked to her side. Gently, I reached out and touched a couple of her fingers, being careful not to disturb any of the medical equipment.

"Mom, you're going to be okay. Dr. Havel has fixed you right up. You're going to wake…" my voice cracked, and a tear rolled down my cheek. "You're going to wake up and we'll talk tomorrow. I'll be here first thing." Slightly squeezing her fingers, I bent over and kissed them. "I love you, Mom."

Dr. Havel stood in the doorway and gently closed the door after I walked through. "She'll be okay Libby. I know it looks bad, but really, I've seen much more serious cases."

"Why are her eyes swollen and black?" I asked as we walked back to the lobby.

"Could be several things. It is normal when we drain to have some pooling of blood—so it's possible that's what happened here. However, it's more likely to have happened during the incident, the fall itself."

My stomach lurched. It seemed like someone had pummeled my mother in a boxing match. *Had she been attacked?* I couldn't help but wonder.

Greg and Shelly guided me back to the group once they saw me emerge from the intensive care unit. I solemnly shared what I'd learned.

"Are you hungry?" Shelly asked.

"Not really."

"We're thinking of going to the diner around the corner since none of us have eaten dinner yet. If you'd like to join, maybe it would be good to be with friends."

The last thing I wanted was food. But I also couldn't

imagine going back home and sitting with my thoughts. Sleep was not in my immediate future, I knew that. I gave her a slight nod and then did it again when both Greg and Lexi gave me that look—*Are you sure?*

* * *

Once out of the hospital and sipping on a chocolate milkshake at the diner, I agreed the decision had been the right one. Mostly I sat around listening to the others, but after a while, I needed to know.

"John—tell me again how you found my mom. From the beginning."

He sat back in the seat, wiping his mouth with a napkin. "Oh man, I keep reliving it. Sure. Well, I was reaching into a box, grabbing some more bubble bath. I was still inside the tent, you know, but uh, near the back of it. There was a noise—couldn't really tell what I'd heard for sure. I kept rummaging through to find this herbal scent Jessica wanted for a customer, and that's when I dropped everything and ran."

"What exactly made you do that?" Greg asked.

"A grunt. Dude, it's hard to describe. Uh, a groan, or thud, or *both*. It was strange. I ran out the side flap and to the back, where I thought the noise had come from. That's when I saw legs kicking outward." We made eye contact again and he quieted, then asked, "Are you sure, Libby?"

I nodded my head.

"I rounded the corner of your mom's tent and saw her passed out."

"But you said her legs were kicking?" Lexi asked.

Bella spoke up. "It's common to have some reflexive,

involuntary movements at the extremities when unconscious."

I smiled. Her EMT training was paying off. "John, did you see anyone else near her?"

"No. No one was around. I immediately called out to Jessica. Margie heard me also and poked her head around the corner."

"When you were in your booth, had you heard anyone talking? Or maybe heard any footsteps running away?"

"Where are you going with this Libby?" Yvette asked pointblank.

John answered, "I don't think anyone was around. But, you know, there's a lot going on there—the background noises are almost constant conversation. I can't say for sure that I heard your mother in one of them. Dang, I just don't know."

I turned to Yvette. "When I went to see Mom, her eyes were dark and swollen. Just wondering when that happened."

John began shaking his head vehemently. "I don't think a fight was going on, if that's what you mean."

"She could have fallen because someone hit her over the head," I simply stated.

His eyes grew wide.

* * *

In the evening's hecticness, I couldn't believe I hadn't called my sister to tell her about our mom. I dialed her number now and retold everything I knew. Instead of being berated for not calling her, she actually said she understood. She also explained it wouldn't have been good for the children. That's when I knew she must have felt similar to me about hospitals and our father's death. It was something we sisters never talked about directly.

By the end of the call, we agreed to go to the hospital together in the morning after the school runs. She'd have Ryan's dad take him for the day. I'd already been relieved of festival duties the next day. The team said they'd cover through the weekend if needed. I let them know we'd see when Mom got released and then I'd make that decision. More importantly, we needed to find help for Margie.

Greg and I tried watching some TV, just to distract my brain. It worked; within minutes, I was asleep.

CHAPTER TWENTY-THREE

The next morning when Jordan and I walked into the hospital, we learned Mom was out of ICU and now in her own room. When we walked in, she was sitting up eating some orange Jello.

"Hey, you two!" Margie said from the seat in the corner. "Your mom has quite the appetite this morning."

I went straight to Mom and gave her a hug. She looked remarkably better than the last time I'd seen her. Still appearing bruised and broken, and she had tubes and wires hooked to beeping machines, but her complexion was pink again and, most importantly, she smiled.

"I guess I had a little fall," she said, perfectly coherent.

I sighed with relief.

"Do you remember anything about it?"

"Well, that's what I keep getting asked! I don't remember a thing."

Margie spoke up. "Well, remember you said you'd talked to some woman, but then couldn't remember much after that?"

"Oh, yeah. I don't remember when that was. Was it before my fall?"

My sister decided we were pushing Mom too hard. I pulled a chair near Margie when Jordan started fussing over Mom. I chuckled as she got the inquisition from my sister about what she'd eaten so far. She puttered around, pouring more water into her cup, straightening her sheets, and asking if the bed position was okay. Mom was fine, but my sister kept trying to adjust it just so.

"Margie, who's running the booth this morning?" I asked.

"Oh, many of the knitting ladies around the valley have come to our rescue. It's such a delight seeing everyone pull together. I'll head over there shortly, but I was so worried about your mother after the ambulance pulled away yesterday."

"And look at her. She's looking good, huh?" I tried to keep it lighthearted, not knowing what the doctor's update would be.

"Has the doctor been in yet this morning, Mom?" I heard Jordan ask.

She shook her head at the same time a nurse walked in. We asked for an update and when we could talk to Dr. Havel. Of course, she wasn't sure about the doctor's schedule, but she read off some numbers from Mom's chart that essentially told us her blood pressure, heart rate, and oxygen levels were all back to normal. Well, we could see that from the blinking machines surrounding us, so that wasn't exactly helpful. I asked her to find out what time would be best for us to meet with the doctor and she left us again.

Margie stood and gathered her things from around the chair. "Julia, I'm happy to see you smiling this morning. Please rest and don't worry—we've got everything covered for the charity work."

They said their goodbyes and then Margie left.

I wasn't sure how much longer I was going to tolerate watching Jordan fuss around. It was getting a bit unnerving. Mom wasn't an invalid, and she certainly wasn't a child. Thankfully, within the hour, the doctor walked in.

"Good morning, Libby," he said, shaking my hand. I introduced him to Jordan.

"Well, Julia … I hear you are chatting with the nurses this morning. I'm Dr. Havel. We met in the emergency room yesterday when I performed your surgery—however, I'm sure you remember none of that."

She smiled at him. "Nice to meet you, doctor."

He opened his laptop, setting it on the counter near the sink. Pulling his stethoscope from around his neck, he approached her, listening to her carotid artery and several other places.

"Any pain this morning?"

"Little headache."

"No stabbing pain? Bright lights or flashing in your eyes?" he asked, shining a bright light into each eye.

"No. Well, other than the one you're flashing at me."

He chuckled. "I see your humor is intact. That's good." He looked directly at me and winked. Walking back to his laptop, he typed up a few notes.

The TV screen turned on behind where Jordan and I stood. We maneuvered around to see what the doctor was doing. He selected a file from his computer and it now showed on the screen for all of us to see.

Using a laser pointer, he pointed to the right side of the image. "Here is where we drilled a microscopic hole," he began.

My stomach churned, and I felt my pulse quicken.

"You can see the pooling of blood—that distinct color—here." He scrolled to a new image. "Now, this is an image we took this morning. Much improved. I'm pleased with the progress. However, I will caution that swelling can return. So, it's extremely important that we keep her for a few days. She needs rest and we need to continue evaluating her. She's on some medications to prevent further swelling and it's best we have her close in the first forty-eight to seventy-two hours for certain."

"How long do you estimate before she can go home?" Jordan asked.

"As long as she continues to show improvement— minimum two days, maybe up to a week. Let's see how it goes."

"When will they remove her bandage?"

"Oh, that's coming off this morning. Just a few stitches—it really was minimal, and we shaved as little of the hair as possible." He appeared to have directed that assurance to our mother.

She looked relieved.

"Okay, ladies, I'll be back tomorrow morning. I generally do my rounds between eight and ten. Until then, she's in expert hands here. Rest easy."

It was Friday morning already. Greg was off work through the weekend. After we left the hospital, I picked him up from the house and we went to our favorite brunch spot nearby. Feeling depleted, I ordered a green juice along with my favorite vegetable omelet, hoping it would lift my spirits a little. Greg dived right into his chicken fried steak, biscuits and gravy platter.

"I'm relieved to hear Julia's doing better this morning. That was scary last night." He took another bite.

I nodded. "She looked remarkably better this morning. The only thing now is how to get her to slow down. To listen to the doctor and rest. My mom doesn't do well with instructions like that when she's feeling well."

Greg snickered and took a sip of his coffee.

My phone buzzed in my purse and I reached in to grab it. The reporter. I excused myself and walked outside the café to take the call.

"Libby, we've got results! I'm headed to the vet's office now, but I just *had* to call and let you know we're making progress."

"They've agreed to share them with you?"

"I pulled a few strings. Yes."

I couldn't imagine how she managed it, but was sure happy to have her help. "Thank you, Rachel. I'll keep my phone nearby. My mom is in the hospital, but I'll try to at least keep it on vibrate while I'm in there."

"Oh, no! What happened?"

I explained and then we agreed to talk more later.

Walking back into the restaurant, I saw Greg typing a text message. He looked up and smiled as I approached.

"Sage would like to have us over for dinner sometime soon," he said, waggling his phone.

"Oh, that's so nice—texting with your new neighbor," I teased. "Hopefully, after this festival is over with."

"Hey, *our* new neighbor!" He caught my side-eye lecture coming and quickly changed direction. "Yep, I'll suggest that—after the festival it is."

We finished our breakfast and popped in at the festival after picking up Shadow from the house. The sun shone brightly, almost too hot for a mid-April day. Lexi, Kathleen, and Sydney were working the booth. Both massage chairs were utilized, fair-goers taking advantage of a nice shoulder rub.

Greg saw Shelly and ventured over to talk to her. I followed Shadow when she pulled me over to the water bowl at the edge of our booth. While she lapped up the cool water, I looked out over the crowd. It was much busier than it had been all week. I caught sight of Sydney chatting with people, then saw a woman approach her. It was that woman! The one who came to our spa claiming to inspect it—what was her name again? Heather. Heather and Bailey were the two Mesa *officials* who we gave the tour to. Looking over her shoulder as she did, the woman pulled Sydney by the elbow and led her between two booths. *What was she doing?*

I gently tugged Shadow's leash. "C'mon, let's take a walk," I mumbled, trying to keep my eyes on Sydney.

As we crossed the street, I realized I couldn't see her any longer. They went between the booths directly across from us—one was a local contemporary artist with canvas paintings and the other was selling local honey. I led Shadow to the left of the artist's booth to find the alleyway behind it. As I neared, I heard voices. Shadow's ears perked, and I gave her leash a yank, whispering *shh*. I gave the hand signal for 'sit' and tried to listen in.

"I already told you that!" Sydney hissed.

"Well, *do more!*" Heather retorted before stomping off.

How did these two know each other? And what exactly was Sydney supposed to be doing? Shadow and I turned and walked back toward the street just in time to see Heather briskly walking away. My head whipped left, then right, scanning the crowd for Sydney. *Where did she go?* Shadow and I turned again for the alleyway behind the booths, speeding through, looking all over for Sydney.

Eventually, we ended up near the food court. Apparently, it was already lunchtime—it was packed. Aside from winding our way around the food truck lines, we dodged the goofy guy on stilts, passed the fire-breather, and glanced at a comedian off on a side street. No sign of Sydney anywhere. We turned back to our booth.

Shadow barked. There she was! In front of our booth, handing out pamphlets.

"Hey Libby! I didn't know you were going to work today. How's your mom?" Sydney asked with her usual perky voice.

"Um, Mom is doing better." Suddenly, I felt silly for chasing after the girl—*what exactly was my question for her?* "Sydney, who was that woman you were talking to?" I pointed across the street where they had been standing ten minutes prior.

Her expression displayed pure confusion. "I don't know who you mean, Libby. You know, I've talked to many people today," she said, with a hint of sarcasm.

"She pulled you behind those booths?" I questioned.

"That didn't happen. I've been here on the street passing these out all morning," she held up the stack of fliers in her hand. "In fact, it's my lunch break. I'm starving."

I stared, watching her disregard me, and walk off into our tent. Shadow barked, looking up at me, as though she expected me to do something about it. "What can I do?"

I heard Sydney asking the other ladies if she could bring anything back for them. When they said no, she came out and pranced right on by us. Shadow gave a low growl, obviously disappointed with me. "What? What exactly do you want me to do?"

Greg saw us and came over. "What's wrong?"

"Sydney lied to me."

CHAPTER TWENTY-FOUR

Before I could explain to Greg, my phone rang. I walked Shadow inside our tent and answered the call. I glimpsed Yvette waving to us just as the tent's side flap closed. Greg stayed outside chatting with her.

"Rachel, what did you learn?"

"Libby, you will not believe this. Two of the sick dogs had xylitol in their systems."

"Xylitol?"

"You know, the fake sweetener that makes everything calorie free. Do you think Pupcakes added that component? It's not on the nutrition label."

"I wouldn't think it's a normal additive for pet food, but I can ask them," I said quietly, pulling the door flap aside and seeing Yvette still standing there talking to Greg.

"Let me call you back."

I stepped outside. Greg and Yvette looked over at me inquisitively.

"Hey, Libby," Yvette greeted. "How's your mom? I was just telling Greg that I'm surprised to see you guys here today."

I gave an update and let her know we're headed back to the hospital soon, but Mom needed her rest, too.

"Yvette, is xylitol a regular ingredient used in any part of pet food manufacturing?"

Her hand immediately flew to her mouth, gasping. "Good God, NO! That will kill a dog!" Then her eyes flew open wider as it dawned on her. "Are you saying xylitol made those dogs sick?"

I nodded my head slowly. "Are the FDA product tests back yet from the festival samples?"

She nodded. "They said nothing about xylitol."

"Maybe you should ask them?"

"Libby, how would xylitol make it into our product? Even traces of it can make a dog very ill."

"And maybe it was only *traces* and that's why these particular dogs didn't die?"

"Oh, shit … this is not good."

Shelly heard Yvette and came out of their booth. "What's going on?"

I filled her in on my call with the reporter, which I inadvertently revealed, not realizing I had.

"You're *working* with the *reporter?*" both of the ladies asked in tandem.

"That's not what's important right now. Plus, technically, you brought in the press to begin with," I pointed out to Shelly. "What's important is that we learn who's responsible for poisoning dogs. I'd say the FDA has overlooked something here."

"Yeah, like the exact thing that will shut our business down!" Shelly yelled.

"Now wait a minute. I know you two are not adding this ingredient to your product. So, *who is? How* were they able to do it—whoever did? We need to dig in deeper. And, for certain, we have to keep Pupcakes & More open."

With some prodding, they agreed to reach out to Bart Littel with the FDA. I wanted to speak to my attorney and see if he could request more video footage—this time, surrounding Pupcakes & More. He'd been so focused on the footage around Zen Zone and Dharma, but what about the other vendors? Also, would we learn anything more about my mother's fall if we had footage near their booth? I wasn't sure how cooperative the festival officials would be, but hoped my lawyer could work his magic contacting the right people.

Greg, Shadow, and I were off. Yvette sprang into action with a call to the inspector.

* * *

Once we got to the parking garage and found our vehicle, I remembered the scene with Sydney and filled Greg in.

"Maybe she really hadn't remembered the woman—I mean, she has been talking to a lot of different people?" he suggested.

"Hon, they were *arguing* about something. You'd remember a confrontation. She's lying, and I want to find out why. I didn't press it back there in front of the rest of the crew, but I intend to get her alone and press her on this."

While Greg drove, I made a few phone calls. First was to check on Mom. She sounded even more lively than earlier that morning, which was such a relief. I told her we'd come by later in the afternoon. Next, I left the message with my attorney, hoping that he'd go ahead with the request for more camera footage without further conversation. Time was running out. At least, it felt that way—there were only three more days of the festival left. If we failed to direct the police and festival officials towards the real culprits, I could be on my way to jail. And Shelly and Yvette could be out of jobs. Also, even though I didn't have concrete evidence yet, my gut feeling was that my mother's fall was more than an accident. None of this sat well with me. I *had* to figure this out, and waiting wasn't exactly my strong suit.

By mid-afternoon, Yvette informed us that the inspector had confirmed the absence of xylitol in every batch at the plant. So now it was clear that someone had tampered with the treats once they were at the festival. *Who had the motive, means, and opportunity to do that?*

Greg and I bantered ideas back and forth. Nothing made sense.

Since Chris hadn't called back yet, we dropped Shadow off at home, and we made our way to the hospital. Mom was in good spirits and only complained of a slight headache. We spent an hour chatting and keeping her company.

"How're the ladies doing at the booth?" she asked.

I assured her everything was going well, and she only needed to rest.

"I can rest at home."

"You heard the doctor. They need to monitor you for

a couple of days."

She rolled her eyes. "I'm fine."

"Have you remembered anything else about your fall?"

She shrugged a shoulder slightly. "I think I remember restocking the shelves. I can't imagine what I'd have done to do all this." Her index finger pointed to her head. "I mean stitches and all. Sheesh!"

"You were knocked out cold, Mom. It seems it was quite a hit to the head. Like someone hit you, pushed you down, or…"

Her eyes widened in confusion. "Who would have hit me?"

Greg stepped in, giving me a look. "Julia, we don't know that anyone did. It's only one theory. Unless you remember getting dizzy? Or, maybe you tripped over something?" he gently suggested.

"I don't remember a thing."

I recalled something Margie mentioned earlier in the morning. "Mom, Margie asked you about a woman you were talking to yesterday. Do you know who she was talking about?"

"Oh, I think she meant one of Sydney's relatives. But, I'm pretty sure that was way earlier, and before this happened." She pointed to her head again.

I remembered meeting the nice knitting club lady who was a relative. That had to be who mom was talking about. I knew for a fact that wasn't someone who'd harm a friend. First, she was super sweet, but also, Ms. Watson was incredibly petite, so much smaller than my mother. I couldn't imagine her being able to harm anyone.

"Was there anyone else?"

"Well, sure there was … Libby, I talked to dozens of

people yesterday!"

"Maybe there's a particular conversation that stands out more than the others?"

"Oh, Libby. Always creating a mystery when there is none. I don't know…" she leaned back, sighing.

That wasn't true. She made it sound as though I always made stories up. She had hit a nerve, and Greg detected it immediately.

Greg touched my arm. "Maybe we should let your mom rest, sweetie?" he asked me.

Which I also took his question to include, *before you two kill each other.*

* * *

On our way across town to the spa, my phone rang. "Chris!"

"Hi, Libby. I got your message and I've already asked the officials I'd worked with previously. Can you meet me at the police station around five this evening?"

"Yes!" I answered immediately, hoping my spa schedule was clear, but deciding it would be.

"I have my boyfriend, Greg with me, if that's okay."

He affirmed.

"Cool. See you then."

I turned to Greg. "He sounded hopeful. Maybe we'll figure this out today!"

Greg pulled into the spa parking lot and we walked in, waving at Bella, who was on the telephone, as we passed by.

"Somewhere here I have the numbers for those veterinarian offices. I'd like to call and question what happens to a dog who may have consumed xylitol. Or how they could even get exposed to it." I rummaged around on the desk and eventually found it.

Greg went to the kitchen to grab us each a soda while I placed the call. By the time he came back, I was pacing the room.

"No one answers calls anymore," I mumbled, my frustration growing. I texted Rachel and asked about her progress.

"We're going to have to be patient, Libs." He tried placating, but patience wasn't in my playbook today, so he turned to using distraction instead. "So, is your schedule cleared for the rest of the day?"

"Oh, right…" I turned on my computer and checked the scheduling app. "I should be finished by four-thirty. That's enough time to get there for the meeting with Chris, right?"

He agreed and gave me a kiss on the way out. He decided to wait for me at home and he'd pick me up later.

It was precisely four-thirty when I found Greg and Shadow waiting for me in the lobby.

"Oh, I didn't know you were bringing my sweet girl," I cooed, petting her. "Hopefully Chris will be alright with it."

"I thought you'd brought her with you previously?"

"I have, but I'm still not sure it's preferred—by Chris or the cops. Oh, well … they'll deal with it."

Shadow gave a little yip and a bounce in agreement.

"Oh wait, I've got to sign out. Hold on." I made my way behind the front desk. Pulling the keyboard tray out, I typed my code to unlock the screen. My eyes scanned over the desk impatiently, while I waited for the software to load, and I caught sight of a Post-it note.

It read: JM—Havel

In smaller writing below I saw: LM fntr

Greg caught me staring at the piece of paper and questioned me.

"I don't think this is Bella's writing. Not sure whose it is—guess Sydney's?"

Greg read the notes and shrugged. "Who knows? Maybe JM-Havel was a reminder to order flowers for your mom? I don't know, but we're going to be late if we don't leave now … did you finish?" He pointed to the computer.

I quickly typed into the app and signed out. Then we were on our way.

* * *

Chris had the video files loaded when we arrived.

First, we watched footage surrounding the Pupcakes & More booth. I had asked specifically for the first day, including setup day. We didn't have twenty-four hours to spend reviewing every minute of footage, but we watched Shelly and Yvette, with the help of two others, erect the booth. The two helpers looked like fairly stout men. I hadn't remembered people helping them set up, but then again, it was a crazy busy day and I felt certain we hadn't met either of the ladies until either late that day, maybe even the next. Jotting down a note to remind me to ask about their helpers, I told Chris to proceed.

We sped up the footage as it played through the night. I was particularly interested in their storage container since we'd seen them put all their products inside it before leaving that evening. We also knew vandalism and theft occurred during that night. We might learn more about who came into our booth and vandalized.

Shadow barked.

"Wait! Stop!" I yelled out, paying attention to the video's time line. "Back up to about thirty-eight ... yeah, right there." Then I looked down at Shadow. *Was that why she barked?* I shook my head, couldn't be.

We slowed the speed and all our eyes watched intently. "There! Stop!"

Chris did a ten second rewind and we watched again.

"Oh, never mind. It's a dog nosing around."

Greg laughed. "Sure enough, look ... he knows where the good stuff is!"

Chris continued and we found nothing else suspicious through the nighttime footage.

Again, my patience was waning. "This could take days. Is there any way you could give us the files? We could each check different ones—you know, divide and conquer," I pleaded.

Chris appeared hesitant, but also seemed to realize the dilemma we were in. "Libby, I'm supposed to keep custody. I'm not allowed..."

"I *promise* not to tell a soul!"

"And, of course, we'd never share with anyone," Greg added.

"I don't know," he whispered, looking behind him at the door.

Suddenly very uncomfortable, remembering we're in a police station, I gave in. I faced him, fixing my eyes pointedly at him. "You know, it's okay, Chris. We understand. Let's keep going—we'll do the best we can."

We spent the next hour with no luck at all.

"Listen, folks. I don't think we're going to find anything

here today. Let's resume later."

"But …"

His hand reached out and squeezed mine. He enunciated carefully, "Really. Let's continue our review *later*." Winking, he removed his hand.

Frustrated, I gave in. "I believe we'll find what we're looking for on that footage, Chris. But, okay, we'll call it a day. When can we meet again?"

"Soon."

He pulled out a thumb drive, closed down the laptop, and bent over to place them in his briefcase. We shut down the TV, rolled the chairs to the table, and turned out the lights. I'd never felt more defeated, but I understood others don't have the same tenacity.

We all walked out of the police station and toward the parking garage. He walked us to our vehicle. While Greg loaded Shadow into the back, Chris leaned toward me.

"Libby, I trust you. Code is lmfest2024. You have twenty-four hours. I'll be in touch." He stared at my purse and also put a finger over his lips. Confused, I watched him walk away.

The car door slammed; Greg came around to the driver's side. "Ready?"

On the way home, I dug through my purse.

I found a thumb drive.

CHAPTER TWENTY-FIVE

We saved footage from Stitches of Love on Greg's computer, and I opened another window on mine watching Pupcakes & More, reviewing it all for hours.

Other than the occasional 'look at this', we had learned nothing truly revealing to this point. Bella came home around seven.

"You two sure are intent on something. Have you even eaten anything?" she asked us. Then coming closer, looking over my shoulder, she asked, "What are you doing? Is that *at* the festival?"

"Yeah, we're trying to get Libby off the cop's radar," Greg mumbled, his eyes fixed on his monitor.

"Well, have you eaten?" she asked again.

We both shook our heads. "I'd eat though ... are you offering?"

"Sure. I can pick something up or we can order in. What sounds good?"

"Pizza is fine. Whatever we normally order—not picky."

She left the room to order pizza and the next hour sped by. Before we knew it, the doorbell rang and our pepperoni and black olive thin crust pizza had arrived.

"Guess it's as good a time as any for a break." I stood and stretched.

I gathered plates and napkins. Greg poured us some wine and Bella grabbed a beer from the fridge. As we sat and devoured the entire pizza, we filled Bella in on the day, including my mom's progress. That's when I remembered.

"Shoot! We told Mom we'd be back this evening!" I checked my watch and it was already after eight. Looking around for my phone, I found it on the kitchen counter. "Let's do a video call." I set it up on my computer to call my mom's phone. We placed the laptop at the end of the table where we could all see.

When she answered, she looked good, but was still patting down her hair. "Oh, Libby. A video call while in the hospital? Really?"

I laughed. "You look fine, Mom."

Bella waved. "Hi Julia! You're looking great! When are you getting out of there?"

"Soon, sweetie … soon."

"Any additional news since we left earlier?" Greg asked.

"No. They just keep taking blood and these darn machines keep beeping."

"Have you gotten any rest?" I wanted to know.

"Barely. I fall asleep and then someone walks in or there's commotion in the hallway. A hospital is not a place for rest, I tell you!"

"Ah, Mom. Maybe only one more night?"

"We'll see." She leaned in. We saw her nose suddenly appear close, becoming enormous and bulbous on the screen. "Hey! Is that pizza I see?"

We all looked around the table to see who would answer.

"Uh, yeah. We just finished a little pizza," I said, sheepishly.

"How dare you! I'm fed hospital food and you're taunting me with pizza!"

Thank goodness she laughed about it. "Sorry, Mom. We just wanted to call before it got much later. Sorry we didn't make it back there this evening."

"Yeah, what's the hold up? Pizza, I see."

"No, no. Bella just brought us this. Greg and I have been working all afternoon and evening." I looked at them to corroborate that. They both nodded.

"Working on what?"

"We're trying to find out who tainted Pupcakes treats."

"Oh?"

"Yeah, we have a video that we're hoping will help. So far, we're striking out, though. Oh! But, we learned earlier that it's xylitol that made at least one dog sick."

"Xylitol? Like as in gum?"

"Sweetener, yeah."

"Oh, dear."

"We're hoping that there is footage of these culprits caught on camera."

"Ugh. Good luck. That sounds tedious."

Greg laughed. "You got that right, Julia."

"How do you let her drag you into these things, Greg?" she asked.

He blushed. "I'm not sure. Guess that's a sign of true love."

Being the next one blushing, I waved them both off. "Oh, stop it, you two. I see what you're doing here."

They both feigned innocence, and we went about chatting for a few more minutes. It was so nice to see my mother laughing and smiling, even if most of the laughter was at my expense. After all, only twenty-four hours earlier, we were so fearful of her prognosis.

Hours later, still scrutinizing footage, Greg startled. Shadow jumped up and barked.

"What is it?" I asked both of them.

"Come here, Libby. Look at this …"

Leaning over his shoulder, I squinted. The Stitches of Love booth cast shadows, making the east side dim in the late afternoon light. My mom was talking to someone near the front corner, closest to the street. I saw my mom's face clearly several times, but the person's back was to us, and kept blocking us from seeing her.

"Female?" I asked Greg.

"Seems so."

For most of the scene, we couldn't see Julia well because the woman was quite large—at least bigger than my mother. I couldn't place her; she seemed familiar, but after all the people we'd interacted with all week, that wasn't surprising.

"Does something happen? Why were you bothered?" I asked him.

"Wait. It's coming…"

Within seconds, I saw the woman's arm fly up in frustration. My mom's expression was disgust. She turned and walked away. The woman followed her, right out of view of the camera.

"Isn't there a camera at the back of the booth? The storage container footage?" I hastily prompted Greg to open a new file.

He floundered, opening the file that was before and after the current one in the listing. Neither were the one. "It doesn't appear these are in any order."

"For Christ's sake!" I slapped my hand down at my side, startling Shadow. She whined and nosed my hand. Regretting that I'd scared her, I took a deep breath. "You probably need outside, don't you?" I asked her. She bolted for the back door—that was my answer.

I stepped out into the cool night breeze and Shadow ran for the other end of the yard to do her business. Standing outside, staring at the stars, I realized how exhausted I felt. I wanted all this to be over: the festival, the investigation, and of course, I wanted my mother healthy and at home. When I walked inside, Greg had come to the same conclusion.

He wrapped me up in a giant hug. "Honey, we can't do all of this in one night. It's late. Let's go to bed; everything will become clearer in the morning."

* * *

He was right. The second my eyes opened the next morning, I knew I had to talk to Shelly or Yvette. I jumped out of bed and found Greg already pouring coffee in the kitchen.

Scanning the room, I asked, "Where'd I leave my purse?"

He pointed to the side table near the sofa. I poked around inside until I found my phone.

"C'mon Shadow, let's go outside," I called out as I pushed the button to call Shelly.

Stepping outside, I breathed in the nice cool air. As I listened to the phone ringing, the sky captivated my attention. Wispy clouds with sunbeams dancing among them created a painting on the blue sky's canvas. When there was no answer on Shelly's phone, I hung up and tried Yvette's. After a few seconds, I realized I would not reach either of them now.

Greg came up from behind, startling me. "Sorry. Here's some coffee. What's wrong? Seem jumpy this morning already."

"I need to talk to Shelly or Yvette. I'm going to get dressed and head down there early. I'll take Shadow with me. Maybe you can continue reviewing the video while we're gone? We shouldn't be long," I asked, hurrying back inside the house.

"Sure," he called out, but I was already down the hallway.

We caught Shelly off guard when we rushed into their Pupcakes booth. Shadow nosed her arm; she jumped, nearly dropping the container she held in her hand.

"Jeez, Libby! What's the hurry?" she asked, holding out the round plastic object. "Mint? Wait, what's wrong?"

Shadow barked.

Absentmindedly, I held my hand out, took a mint, and popped it into my mouth. Shadow jumped up and bumped my elbow, barking wildly. "Shadow! What are you doing?" Then I realized. My eyes flew open and I spit the mint back out into my hand. "Shelly, can I see that packaging?"

She held up the mint container. "This? What's wrong? Are they stale?" She handed it over, looking baffled. Slowly, she also removed the mint from her mouth, staring at it suspiciously.

I found the ingredient list and sure enough, it listed xylitol and several other similar 'tol' additives: sorbitol, maltitol, as well as aspartame, etc. Gasping, I met Shelly's eyes again, "This could be the culprit."

"What are you talking about, Libby? You're scaring me."

We both threw our mints into the nearby garbage can.

Yvette popped her head into the tent. "Oh hey, Libby … just saw you tried to call. Sorry I missed it. What? What's wrong, you two?"

"Get in here," I waved Yvette inside. "Yesterday, we learned xylitol made a dog sick. Look at the ingredients here." I handed over the sugar-free mint packaging to Yvette. "I'll bet you any word that ends with 'tol' is also a form of xylitol. We'll get someone to confirm that for us, but regardless, the bad stuff is in these mints."

"Okay. But that doesn't explain how that makes Pupcakes treats responsible, does it?"

"I beg to differ. I think this explains exactly why you guys are *not* responsible for those dogs becoming ill! That's the point!" I excitedly explained. "Mom mentioned something about gum yesterday when I told her what we'd learned on the sugar-free additive. Then fast forward to today. Shelly handed me the mint, and I knew. Somehow, the dogs had to have come in contact with something like mints or gum or artificial sugar. I mean, it's highly unlikely someone is carrying around xylitol in its purest form, right?"

"I always have these mints around," Shelly started, looking horrified. "What if there was some cross-contamination with an open bag, and the treats we handed out to passing customers? That would still make us responsible! Oh, I couldn't bear..." she cried out.

As she said it, I remembered finding a mint canister on the ground one day at the back of their tent. I had thought nothing of it at the time. Could dogs have gotten hold of mints, eaten them, and become sick? As I recalled, the container I picked up wasn't all chewed up, so that didn't seem likely.

Yvette stepped in. "Oh, that's just silly. How on earth would the cross contamination happen, Shelly?"

She thought about it for a second. Her eyes flew open. "Or, what if *someone else* tampered with the product, adding *these*," she shook the mints, "to an open package?"

Now we were thinking along the same lines. *What if the container I found that day was actually evidence left behind from someone who'd done the tampering?* "You could be on to something, Shelly. It would make sense—how there were only a few dogs, versus potentially dozens more, affected. The sample size was relatively small."

"And with only the two of us running the booth, there could have been plenty of opportunities for someone to slip into the back there without us noticing," Yvette added, pointing at the very back of their booth. Exactly where I'd found the mint package.

Remembering that Greg was still reviewing camera footage, I had a thought. "Or did they get into your container overnight?"

"If that were the case, I think more product would have been affected."

True. Then I remembered why I'd come there in the first place, before Shadow's barking and the mints distracted me, so I filled them in about Greg and me reviewing a video with my attorney yesterday. Without elaborating on the complete story, keeping my promise to Chris about the thumb drive, I told them about watching the footage surrounding their booth.

"During setup, you had two men helping. I haven't seen them around here since, so I'm guessing they weren't employees. Can I ask who they are? Do you know them personally, or were they hired help?"

Yvette immediately chimed in. "We used the suggested hired help the festival officials provided."

That was news to me. I wasn't aware they offered such a service.

Shelly asked, "Why? Who'd you use?"

"Greg and JJ."

They both nodded their heads.

"Any concerns about them?" I asked.

They looked at each other and then back at me. Both shook their heads. Yvette added, "They performed the job they were hired to do. As I remembered, both were pleasant enough. Nope, no issues."

"Okay. Well, if you don't mind, I'm going to take these mints and hopefully we can get the veterinarians to do some more testing. Think Bart Littel will be of help, if we asked?"

"I'll call him," Shelly offered.

"Thanks, ladies! I'll be back later." Before I forgot, I quickly texted Rachel, asking about progress with the vets.

"Oh, how is your mom doing?" Yvette asked me before I turned to leave.

"I'm heading over there shortly, but last night, she was doing fine. Well, irritated that we hadn't brought her pizza." I rolled my eyes.

They both laughed. "Sounds like she'll be just fine."

Back at the house, I filled Greg in on the conversation with the ladies. He had found the footage with their storage locker, but had nothing more to report. Before it got much later, we needed to be at the hospital for the doctor's rounds, so we left Shadow with a cookie and hopped into Greg's truck.

Mom was in rare form, demanding to be set free today. Thankfully, the doctor's update was good. The most recent scans showed no further swelling. The nurses had Mom up and walking around the hallways and she did spectacularly. No dizziness and after a couple laps, her strength was rebounding.

"So long as your blood tests from this morning check out, I will sign off on your release by late afternoon. You're doing great, Ms. Madsen!" Dr. Havel smiled, asking if we had questions, and then he was off to finish his rounds.

"You heard him though, right? You still need to take it easy, Mom. No festival work!"

She grinned. "I'll rest today."

"And, tomorrow …"

"We'll see."

As we walked out of the hospital, I got the call from Rachel.

CHAPTER TWENTY-SIX

Sure enough, Rachel had confirmed with each veterinarian that xylitol was the weapon in this particular crime. Now we needed to figure out who brandished said weapon and harmed the dogs, as well as Pupcakes & More's reputation. *Did we actually know someone set out to harm anyone? What if this happened by accident?* Dogs found the mints, carelessly left lying around, and they ate them. I pictured the footage Greg and I saw of a random dog skulking around at night. Then, I also remembered the vandalism—the warning message that still occupied our booth's floor, underneath the rug. The one that said, distinctively: GO AWAY! And what about the booths that were torn down the first night? The products stolen from multiple vendors. *None of this happened by accident.*

Before Rachel hung up, I wanted her to have the information about the two men who set up the Pupcakes & More booth. She said she'd run those leads down. Thankfully, she never questioned what camera footage I referred to.

We picked up sandwiches at Subway, and by the time we got back to the house, I was ready to sit and review the video again. We spent the rest of Saturday afternoon doing just that. A couple of hours later, I groaned.

Greg perked up. "What did you find?"

"Oh, no, I just remembered something. That's all." I set down my teacup. "I need to talk to Lexi about Sydney. She boldfaced lied to me yesterday—I'll give Lexi a call, I think she's at the spa by now, and I need a break anyway." I grabbed my phone and took Shadow outside.

When I came back in, Greg called me over to look at his screen.

"Is this Sydney right here?"

I hovered over his shoulder. "What day was this?"

"Yesterday. It might be the lady she was talking to?"

"It is. That's exactly it! And, look, right there…" The woman turned where I got a good look at her face. "That's the city worker! Heather."

Greg zoomed in. "I wish these cameras had audio."

"But regardless, doesn't it appear they are familiar with each other? I don't think—and I didn't yesterday either—it was some passing customer Sydney started talking to!"

"So hard to know without hearing the conversation, but yes, I agree with you. As a bystander, I'd think they knew each other well."

"Is there a way to save this one clip separately? I'd like to show it to Lexi—this supports exactly what I just told her."

"Let me see how the security is set up here."

"I'll get you another thumb drive." I ran to the bedroom and grabbed one from my drawer.

Within seconds, he handed it back to me with the clip saved.

"Let's go, Shadow!" I grabbed her leash. "I'd rather get some exercise than drive over to work. We'll be back soon." I kissed Greg on the top of his head, then my dog and I ran out the door.

Lexi was in the office when we breathlessly stopped in the doorway.

"Did you just run here?" she asked.

Trying to catch my breath, I nodded. "Yep."

I held up a finger, ran to the kitchen, and grabbed a bottle of water. When I returned, I sat down in a chair and Shadow flopped down on my feet.

"You're the only one here today," I commented. "Someone should be here with you."

"They're still around, over there in PT. It's okay." She pushed her keyboard tray away, resting her elbows on the desk and leaning toward me. "What are you doing here?"

I pulled the thumb drive from my pocket, waggling it. "You need to see this." I handed it to her and she plugged it into her computer, selecting the one file on the drive.

"This is Sydney? What are you doing filming her?"

"This came from the cameras that are set up at the festival. They're all around—but mostly along the vendor rows. I've been studying them to clear my name on the Zen Zone theft, as well as helping Shelly and Yvette."

"Okay. And what does that have to do with Sydney?"

"I'm not sure yet. But, as I told you on the phone, I know she lied to my face yesterday. This is proof."

"Oh! This is the lady you saw her with and she denied

talking to?"

"Yes."

Lexi leaned in closer, squinting at her monitor. "Hey…"

Knowing my friend well, I nodded. "Yes, I think so…"

"The lady to whom we gave a tour?"

I nodded again.

"So she knows her?"

"Well, she lied to me, but yes, that's my assumption based on what I saw. On this. Until I can talk to her, I don't actually know. But Greg and I think that's obvious in this footage, don't you think?"

She nodded slowly, using her mouse to replay the clip.

"Lexi, they both ran from me and then later, when I questioned Sydney, she gaslit me. Why?"

"Do you have a theory?"

"Not specifically—about her. However, we haven't been able to get hold of those two city permit officials yet, including the one in the video. I mean, we still have questions about their visit, right? Why are they being so cagey—so difficult to talk to? If Sydney knows this one, let's see how we can get hold of her."

"Okay, let's question Sydney then." She clicked her mouse and opened a new application. "She's scheduled to be here tomorrow morning—but it looks like you're scheduled at the booth?"

"Diane is covering. Since Mom's hospitalization."

"That's right. Okay. Let's confront her and find out what she's hiding."

"Oh! I nearly forgot!" I signaled for Lexi to follow me, and we went to the front lobby. I walked behind the desk and pulled out the keyboard tray. "There were a couple of notes here." Today the desk was completely clean. No notes anywhere.

"What did they say?"

"One was JM and also written next to it was my mom's doctor's name. The other I can't remember, except it had what could have been my initials—LM."

"And what do you think it meant?"

"I don't know. Do you have examples with Bella's writing compared to Sydney's?"

"What exactly are you trying to prove, Libby?" She laughed. "This desk belongs to both of them and I'm sure they both take notes."

"Yeah, you're right. And I can ask Bella when she gets home."

"I'm just curious—do you suspect Sydney of something? I mean, other than lying about talking to that woman?"

Beginning to feel a little silly and not knowing exactly what I suspected, I only shrugged and brushed it off for now. I probably was blowing everything out of proportion, but regardless, Sydney had lied to me. She was our employee, and I needed assurance that I could trust her. Once I explained it that way to Lexi, she reaffirmed the need for a meeting the next morning. In the meantime, Shadow and I could use a little more cardio before getting back to reviewing the video.

* * *

When we walked in the door, Greg was on the phone. I went straight into the bedroom, looking for the pair of yoga pants I'd been wearing earlier in the week. On our run, I remembered I'd shoved a couple scraps of paper into the small pocket. One was Bella's notation of our client's phone number—the man I still hadn't reached to ask about the message he'd left. The other was that actual message found on the massage table. There was something familiar that I couldn't quite place; I needed to see it again and maybe it would trigger the memory.

Greg walked through and nearly got hit by clothing. "Whoa, what are you doing?"

"Sorting laundry?"

"Looks a little more intense than that to me."

With my head farther into the laundry hamper, I mumbled, "They are in here somewhere." When I came up for air, I asked, "Have you seen those maroon and gray patterned yoga pants?"

"You have a thousand pairs of yoga pants. Can't you wear something else today?"

"That's not the point. I need something in the pocket of that specific pair."

"Oh, okay. Here, let me help you. Maybe they aren't in the hamper?" He went into the closet. Several seconds later, he came out. "These?" He held up the pants.

"Yes!" I snatched them away and shoved a hand into the deep side pocket meant for a cell phone. Unfolding the folded-up paper, I stood staring at them.

"Find what you needed?"

"Yep, all good." I carried the notes out into the living room, found my purse, and slid them inside. Seeing them hadn't triggered a memory, but I felt sure I'd want them handy. There was something unsettling about them; I'd figure it out.

Greg and I went back to the records we'd each made from reviewing the video. We questioned several things.

First, the woman speaking to mom the day of her fall—who was she? I thought it was Heather, but could I say for certain? Maybe Mom would eventually remember. Also, we discovered two men that had helped at Pupcakes. Hopefully, Rachel would track them down. Then, we knew that Jessica from Zen Zone, Sydney, and I all were of similar height and weight. When fully covered, you couldn't tell any of us apart. At least not on grainy nighttime camera footage. Chris seemed to think that was enough to keep me from going to jail. Or was it?

By the time our eyes couldn't take anymore screen time, we decided to get out of the house. I noticed several texts from Chris—I knew our time limit with the video was nearly up, but we needed just a little longer. I called the hospital; Mom wasn't ready for release yet, and she wasn't a happy camper. It was early evening, so I suggested we stop by the booth to check in with the closing crew. They might need the help; I hadn't exactly offered much assistance the past two days. We grabbed Shadow's leash and headed to downtown Mesa.

The Saturday evening crowd was rowdier than they'd been during the week. Loud music blared, the aroma of food filled the air, people drinking when we passed the beer gardens, lots of laughter, and children running around everywhere. It was festive and lively.

Passing the man on stilts, Greg said, "I don't know how he does that."

"I know! Makes me uncomfortable." I laughed, and then caught sight of the magician pulling something out of a box. He had an enormous crowd around him. "These street performers have amazing energy. They've been going at it all week long."

"They must make good tips."

We walked up to the booth as Bella and Kathleen were chatting with customers. Shadow wiggled up to Bella, and she took her leash, giving the pup a good rubdown at the same time. Greg and I walked inside the booth.

"Want us to help load the container?" I hollered.

Bella gave a thumbs up.

Within half an hour, all our product was in the container and our tent flaps tied. Bella and Kathleen said goodbye; I watched as they disappeared into the crowd.

"I'm hungry. Think we have time for one of those huge turkey legs?" Greg asked.

I chuckled. His face looked like I imagined it did when he was eight years old, asking his mother a similar question. "Yeah. Mom hasn't called yet. But, hey … why don't you go on over there? I'm going to head down the lane and check in with Margie. Come back here—or I'll text if I finish first and we'll meet up in between."

"Sounds good," he gave me a peck on the cheek.

Darkness had settled in and I noticed the street lights on our row hadn't kicked on quite yet. It was still enough to see with light glowing from the vendor tents, but I worried about Margie and the older ladies. We wouldn't want to risk another fall.

As we made our way down the street, it appeared Stitches of Love was already closed down. We continued, hoping they weren't floundering in the dark near the storage. Shadow spooked and let out a growl.

"What is it?" Her hackles spiked along her back; her ears pressed down and nose pointed forward. Still growling, she pulled me. "Shadow? What's wrong?"

We turned between Mom's booth and Zen Zone. John

and Jessica were nowhere around. The Stitches of Love booth appeared empty when I quickly peeked inside one flap. Everything was dark, with all neighbors closed already. This portion of vendor row was quiet, even though I could still hear the thumping of music and a crowd in the background. I examined the lock on their container and found it latched tight.

Shadow suddenly lost it and barked with imminent warning. I spun around, hearing footfalls nearby.

Grabbing my phone from my pocket, I fumbled to find the flashlight. Pointing it straight in front of me, I whirled around, checking our surroundings. I caught a glimpse from beneath the flaps from the booth—someone *had* been in the booth.

We ran around the other side where they'd escaped. Shadow pulled hard, twisting me around, and I fell, unable to hold on to her. "Shadow!" She ran off into the darkness. I jumped right up and took off running after her.

Ahead, I saw someone dart off between vendor booths, headed toward the crowds about a block away. The black outline of Shadow's figure dashed to catch her prey. I gave it all I had and never saw the curbing, tumbling forward, reaching out to break my fall, with numerous expletives flying from my mouth as I rolled to a stop.

"Shadow!" I yelled out, knowing it was a futile effort.

Footfalls were closing in.

"Here, let me help you," a man's voice jolted me upright, scaring the hell out of me.

My heart pounded. I started screaming. "Leave me alone! What do you want with me?!" I screamed out, hoping vendors would come to my rescue.

"Libby, let me help you up." I recognized the voice and

was confused.

"Chris?"

"Yes. You took quite the fall—are you okay?"

The drumbeat pounding my brain was relentless. I couldn't comprehend why my attorney was standing over me.

"What are you doing *here*?" I stressed the question.

"Here, let me help you up." He held out a hand. I attempted to take it, but grimaced. "Want me to call for help?"

"Just give me a minute." I tried taking a deep breath. "Did you see which way Shadow ran?"

"I'm sorry, I didn't see your dog."

"Did you see the person running? The one we were chasing?"

"No. I was about to ask you why you were running. Libby, you know this doesn't look good. Why are you lurking around the booths at night when they're closed?"

I couldn't do this with him right now. I turned over to my hands and knees. Even though everything in my body screamed painfully, I carefully rose and walked it off.

"What are you doing here, Chris? You haven't answered me."

"I need the thumb drive. Remember, twenty-four hours? Well, it's been more than that now."

"Really? You're chasing me down for a thumb drive?"

"I wasn't chasing anyone!"

Frantically remembering Shadow got away, I snapped at him. "I don't have time for this! I've got to find my dog!" Then, feeling horrible for lashing out, I apologized. "I'm sorry, Chris. Today got away from me; I fully intended to return the flash drive. And then—*this*..." I brushed dirt off my pant legs. "Listen, I don't have the flash drive here, but I promise to get it to you. Right now, I really need to find Shadow." I began hobbling along, looking for an opening between booths that would lead me back to our vendor row. Chris followed, taking my arm, helping to balance me so we could move quicker.

When we turned the corner, I saw Greg in the distance. In one hand, a huge turkey leg. In the other, he was holding Shadow with her leash. He saw me staggering along and gave Chris an inquisitive look.

"Greg, you remember my attorney, Chris?"

The forest ranger glared at the lawyer before turning his attention on me. "What happened, Libby? Are you okay?"

"I'm glad Shadow found you," I quietly said.

"Yeah, that was really strange. I saw her running through the crowd. I followed, calling her name. Finally, she turned and came to me."

"Did you see who she was chasing?"

"Some kid, I think? Hard to tell, appears everyone's wearing black hoodies tonight."

Greg turned to Chris. "What are you doing here?"

I chimed in. "He's here for his thumb drive; we're past our deadline." I hung my head, now feeling embarrassed. "Shadow pulled me down. Somehow Chris saw us and came running."

Chris must have detected the uncertainty in my retelling of the story. He cleared his throat. "Look. I texted several times earlier, then thought I'd stop by here—figured it's where you'd be. On my way down this aisle, I thought I saw you over by your mom's booth. Walking up the street over there," he pointed, "I followed."

Both Greg and I stood staring, waiting for him to continue.

"And, then you started running. I thought you were running away from me, Libby."

"Did you ever think to call out my name or anything?"

"I did!"

"I never heard you!"

"Yeah, I realize that now. What the heck is going on here? Who were you chasing anyway?"

"Someone was in my mom's booth and I wanted to ask questions. I'm tired of these thugs getting away with stealing."

"Libby, you can't take the law into your own hands," Chris gently said. "You'll get hurt."

We all had a little chuckle over that one. I held my hands out and Greg examined the scrapes.

"Let's get you home and cleaned up, sweetie."

"I need that thumb drive!" Chris reminded us as we walked away.

Before we got to the truck, my phone rang and reminded me of all the missed texts from Chris. He wasn't lying about that. The phone call was from the hospital, and Mom was ready to be picked up, so we drove straight there.

As soon as we stepped into the bright lights in the hospital, I saw exactly how badly my hands and arms were beat up. When we walked into Mom's room, seeing the looks on both hers and the nurse's face told me everyone thought I'd been in a fight.

"What on earth, Libby?" my mom exclaimed.

"Just had a little tumble earlier," I mumbled. I snuck a peek in the mirror and saw that my face had some blood on it. Great, hopefully the bruising would be minimal.

The nurse came over. "Let me see," she said, gently taking my hand and examining all my contusions. "That was some fall." She was so sweet, offering to help clean it up, even though I wasn't her patient. Mom and Greg visited while the nurse tended to my wounds, glancing over when I cried 'ouch'.

Soon we were on our way and Mom interrogated me all the way to her home. Yep, she was feeling better, that was for sure.

CHAPTER TWENTY-SEVEN

By the time Bella came home later that night, I required a couple of Advil and a glass of wine to dull the aching body. She, too, winced when she saw the bandages and bruising that was already forming. After telling her about finding someone sneaking around Mom's booth again, I remembered the papers in my purse.

"Can you hand me my purse? It's on the kitchen counter."

When she did, I pulled out the notes and asked if she'd written either one of them.

"Nope, not my handwriting. But this one looks similar to Sydney's." She inspected it closer. "Well, at least this one for sure ... see how she does her Gs? She does a similar thing with J—an extra curlicue."

She was talking about the note that I'd found on the massage table. My head throbbed. *What was she saying? Sydney wrote the note—not the client?*

"Why, Libby? What's wrong, and what does 'barking up the wrong tree' mean anyway? I mean, besides metaphorically."

I ignored the questions. "Are you sure, Bella? This is Sydney's writing?"

"Oh yeah. Here, I'll be right back!" She ran off to her room. When she came back, she was carrying a different brightly colored Post-it. "See here."

I took it from her. It was the note that I'd seen previously: JM — Havel

"She wrote this one, too?"

"Yes, it was a note to me. I'd asked her to call the hospital—we wanted to send Julia flowers. Only problem was, she hadn't got the room number. So later I called back and ordered them myself. You can see where I wrote down 502 right there."

"Thank you, Bella." The two handwriting styles were distinctively different.

Thankfully, her phone rang in the distance and she ran off to find it. This added yet another thing to discuss with Sydney the next morning, and I wanted to keep Bella out of it. No need to tip off the young receptionist before we got to her.

Turns out, we were too late.

The next morning, when Lexi and I arrived at the spa, Sydney wasn't there. At fifteen minutes past her starting time, we tried calling. No answer.

I presented Lexi with the note that had been left for me days earlier in the therapy room.

"Why hadn't you told me this sooner?"

"Honestly, with everything, I'd forgotten."

"And you think Sydney wrote the note? Why?"

"I *know* she wrote it. Bella confirmed that last night." I displayed the two pieces of paper side by side. "And, why? I can't even rationalize. But that gut feeling I had about her lying to me—well, this doesn't make it any better."

"Wow. I'm trying to wrap my head around this, Libby."

"You and me both."

"Do you think she has something to do with the festival theft? Or, oh crap, *poisoning* dogs?"

"I sure hope not. But someone needs to explain this note, this *threat*. We need to find her and get some answers."

We both picked up our phones. I called Kathleen— she hadn't seen her, and she asked Bella, who was standing nearby. She hadn't talked to her since the day prior. Lexi called Sydney's number again and left a message, trying to sound nonchalant, saying we were worried about her being late for work. Then I remembered Sydney's grandmother was one of the knitting ladies. I called the one person who'd know how to find her.

"Mom, does Sydney's grandmother live close to you?" I asked.

"Oh yeah, just down the street. Why?"

"I need to pay her a visit. You don't happen to have her house number, do you?"

I could hear her walking through her house. "It's here somewhere. Oh, right here! Same street as mine—908 is the house number."

Before she could ask any more questions, I hurriedly said thanks and hung up. Then I called Bella.

"She still hasn't shown up, has she?" Bella said when she answered my call.

"We're worried, Bella. It's not like her. Do you know where she lives?" As I asked her the question, I slapped my hand to my forehead. We have her personnel files. I could have looked it up without involving Bella.

"Yeah, I agree. It's not like her. She lives over off of Greenfield." She gave me the details, which worked out being faster than looking it up. I knew right where to go.

"Okay, thanks a million." I hung up, explaining to Lexi where we were going, as I clipped Shadow's leash on.

We took Lexi's vehicle today—which was actually her husband, JJ's. Neither of us thought Sydney had seen it before, so maybe we'd be successful with the element of surprise. As we drove through her neighborhood, I noticed many driveways were empty. Either people were at work, or they parked in their garages. I hoped that Sydney's little red VW bug would be sitting outside, signaling she was home.

There's a reason they say hope is not a strategy. It rarely works out. We drove slowly past the vacant-looking home a couple times before parking one house down and across the street.

"Why aren't we parking right in front of her house?" I asked.

"She's not answering her phone for a reason. I think we need to be careful."

I giggled. My friend sounded more like me all the time.

We got out and casually walked the dog down the sidewalk on one side, then crossed the road and slowed way down as we approached Sydney's place. The neighborhood was silent.

"Let's just go to the door and knock," I whispered.

Lexi nodded, and we slowly approached the door, both

of us looking to see if the closed curtains moved at all. We stood quietly listening; no sounds coming from inside. I rang the doorbell. No dogs. We waited, observing each window for movement.

"No one is home," I finally said.

"What if she had an emergency? Shouldn't we try to get in and see if she's passed out on the floor?"

"I'm not sure the police would see it that way. She's a young woman—do we *really* have reason to believe she's in danger?"

Lexi pulled out her phone, trying Sydney's number again. We heard nothing from inside so either it was on silent or not here at all.

"I have another place to check. Over by Mom's house, her grandma lives on the same street."

"Okay, let's go."

We ran across the street and loaded in the car. As we drove away, I swore I saw movement in a window. Or was my friend making me more paranoid? I couldn't be sure. We went on to find the grandmother's house.

CHAPTER TWENTY-EIGHT

Ms. Watson was adorable, the consummate hostess, especially when two unannounced visitors showed up at her door. She welcomed us inside with no hesitation, even with the dog. I suspected my mother must have called ahead.

"Can I get you some tea?" she offered.

We both started shaking our head, but she was already pouring from the kettle on the stove.

"Please, please. Have a seat."

We each sat on the sofa and within moments had a tea service set down on the table in front of us. I noticed all the needlework that adorned the room. From candle sconces on the wall, to upholstered chairs, the doilies on the coffee table, and blankets that draped the arms of the couch.

"Have you seen Sydney today?" I asked.

"Oh no, I would have thought she'd be at work."

"She didn't show up, Ms. Watson," Lexi stated.

"Shirley. No need for formalities."

"Shirley, you wouldn't know where we could find her, would you?"

Slowly shaking her head, "Well, she's always with Bailey. But now that they live together, hmmm … I guess Bailey might know best." She told us how the two girlfriends met in the first grade and had been close ever since. She told of all the times the two would spend at her house, baking cookies, and learning to crochet. Before we knew it, she had covered most of their childhood with story after story.

My knee jittered impatiently, waiting for the opportunity to slow down the family history lesson, when something occurred to me. Bailey wasn't a common name.

"I'm sorry to interrupt, Ms., er, Shirley. I'm curious— what's Bailey's last name?"

Lexi's eyebrow raised.

Shirley's eyes cast upward, thinking. "Gee. I know it … but this brain. Well, it has a hard time recalling things some days."

"That's okay. It's probably nothing, but I thought for a moment I may have met her somewhere. Same age as Sydney, right?"

"Oh yes … early twenties. My how the years fly by," she said wistfully. "I know her last name … c'mon brain. Work." She knocked her forehead with her knuckles.

"Well, maybe it'll come to you later."

Lexi asked if she could use the restroom, and Shirley pointed her down the hallway.

My phone rang and I quickly grabbed it from my

pocket to silence it. "Sorry."

"No worries. Take the call. I'll get us more tea."

Before I could stop Shirley, she had the teacups in hand and was en route to the kitchen. I punched the button on my phone.

"Hi Rachel," I answered.

"Libby, I've got names for you. I haven't contacted them yet, but still trying. They are brothers—last name is Young. Eric and Luke. It's a long story, but I didn't find this information from the festival officials. They told me they don't offer such services—the setup has always been the responsibility of each vendor. Of course, for electrical work, they will bring in the professionals. But definitely not to set up a booth. More later—still running down these names. Call you soon."

Interesting. Who hired them, then?

Lexi walked in and questioned the look on my face.

"We didn't have a choice of booth setup personnel, right?"

"No. Up to the vendors to do that. Remember we used our guys for that muscle…"

"Yeah. Just strange. Shelly and Yvette claim the officials provided them with a crew. Rachel confirmed the officials do not provide the service. Something isn't adding up."

"Well, aren't they special? They didn't offer us that!"

"She's going to call me back—two men: Eric and Luke Young were the ones who set up the Pupcakes booth. I'd like to talk to them."

Shirley rounded the corner with a tray and teacups. "That's it! Young. Bailey Young."

Lexi's eyes went wide. "Bailey Young was the assistant from the permit office…"

"Shirley, does Bailey have brothers?"

"Oh yes. Two older brothers—have to be five and seven years older, maybe?"

This was way more than coincidence. My mind whirred, blocking out Shirley's dialogue as she continued chattering. Lexi and I sipped our tea politely for fifteen minutes longer, but only long enough to not appear rude.

"We're really sorry, Shirley. We could sit here all day talking to you! But we're due back at work, so unfortunately, we're going to have to say goodbye."

She thanked us profusely for coming by and visiting. We waved as we pulled away from her driveway.

"Where now?" Lexi asked.

"Does Diane have work covered at the spa?" I asked, while scrolling through text notifications. My attorney was still looking for me.

She nodded, looked both ways, and then pulled out into traffic on Power Road.

"Let's go by my house, if that's okay."

No questions. She drove straight there.

We surprised Greg by walking in the front door.

Standing up from his place at the table where he'd been staring at his laptop, he greeted, "Hello, ladies! Good to see you, Lexi!"

"Find anything new?" I asked, pointing at the screen.

"Not really."

"What are you guys doing?" Lexi walked closer to the computer screens.

"We're not supposed to share, but..." I filled her in on how we came into possession of the video and what we'd been doing. Then she and I filled Greg in on our findings at Ms. Watson's home.

"Wow. And now, knowing that Bailey and the booth setup men are related—that must hold some significance, right?" Greg asked.

"It sure doesn't seem coincidental. But how it all fits—that's what we need to learn next. I mean, if they all work for the city, maybe it's not that suspicious, right?"

Lexi shrugged and pointed out, "We still need to talk to Sydney. What's she lying about? Is she covering something for her roommate?"

"That's right ... they *are* roommates."

We still had our work cut out for us.

CHAPTER TWENTY-NINE

It wasn't much later that evening when we piled into our vehicles and headed back downtown. All hands on deck—we needed everyone's help to take apart and load everything. Except for the actual booth disassembly which would take place Monday morning—the officials were specific about that—we decided instead of leaving the product inside the container overnight we'd take it back to the spa tonight. The sun had just dipped below the horizon and I believe we each felt the same sentiment by now. We were ready to be done with the festival.

"So, Sydney never showed up for work? She never called in?" Diane asked me, as we each took an end of one of the massage chairs, placing it into the back of Greg's Tundra.

"Nope. Never heard a word from her all day." I would not get into the details with another employee, but we really needed to talk to Sydney.

I hustled back to the tent and helped Greg with the shelving unit. When we tilted it, something fell. The sunglasses! I'd never found their owner, which also reminded me I'd planned on asking Margie specifically where she found them.

"Bet you're happy to have this over with?" Greg asked Lexi, as she helped steady the load on the way to the truck.

"I have mixed feelings. It was great to get out of the office all week. We gained quite a few new clients from the special we offered. But, all the drama? Yep, I'm more than happy to leave that behind. Not sure I'd do all this again."

After all the larger pieces were out, I lifted the mandala area rug. We stared at the message displayed in black spray paint: Go Away!

Bella and I stepped forward, kneeling down for closer inspection. We turned to each other, mouths gaping open. We both knew *exactly* who wrote this message.

Before she said anything out loud, I signaled quietly for her not to. As we stood, I whispered, "Keep this between us." We went about folding the large rug and securing it in the truck.

Shelly and Yvette saw our team huddled outside the tents once we finished.

"You guys are efficient!" Yvette commented. "You know we don't have to tear down until tomorrow."

Lexi smiled. "No better time than the present. Greg and JJ will be here early to dismantle the booth. Then we're all done with this place."

"You can use the festival maintenance people to help with that, you know," Shelly said.

"About that—" I turned and asked if I could speak privately with the two of them once we finished. They agreed, said goodbyes to the other ladies, and then went back to their booth.

Lexi and I thanked our crew for all their hard work. We'd already decided to cater a nice luncheon one day in the upcoming weeks for the employees as a celebration for gaining so many new clients.

When Greg, Lexi, Shadow, and I found the Pupcakes ladies again, they too were boxing up product.

"You all are smart," Shelly said. "We decided we'll get our product out tonight, too. Why leave it for some hoodlums to steal, right?"

"About that. We've learned the festival doesn't have a teardown team. Those men who helped you set up at the beginning very well may be involved in sabotaging your business."

"What?" Yvette puffed out her chest, ready to fight.

Before they got too worked up, I revealed what we knew. Particularly, I explained how it seemed like our fake inspectors and their pseudo handymen were related.

"How do you know all this, Libby?"

"Remember, innocent until proven guilty. We have solved nothing yet—especially the *why*, but as soon as we know more, you'll be the first we call."

"Hey, you were going to talk to the inspector…" Greg mentioned.

"Right. I've put in several calls. Nothing back yet though," Shelly explained.

"Okay. Call me if you learn anything new. And ladies, the best part of working at the festival this year was getting to meet you two." I reached out to hug Yvette.

"Oh, you're so sweet, Libby. Lexi. Greg," Shelly said as she made her rounds with hugs and kisses. "Us too. And we hope we can keep in touch and get together occasionally."

After promising again to keep them updated, the three of us left.

At home, Bella was unnerved.

"Sydney is involved, isn't she?" she blurted out the second we walked into the living room.

I gave a shrug and a nod all at once. "I'm not completely sure about anything, but you agree, that was her handwriting, wasn't it?"

She nodded her head slowly.

"Have you tried calling her today?" I asked.

"No, I haven't."

"Maybe she's avoiding our calls, but as her friend, think she'll answer yours?"

"Worth a try, I guess." She ran off to her room, looking for her phone. When she came back in the room, she showed me her missed calls. "Look! She's tried to get hold of me. Oh wait, look here…"

She opened up her text messages; there were a few from Sydney. All of them asked her to call ASAP. She dialed nervously.

"Don't sound alarmed—keep it casual." I quickly whispered.

"Sydney!" Bella held up her finger for me to be quiet. "Where were you today?" The young woman's face changed suddenly. "Sydney? What's wrong? Sydney!" She listened intently and then hung up.

"What is it?" Greg asked.

"She's in trouble. Something is really wrong."

"What did she say?"

"She sounded muffled—maybe even gagged. Said something like—*hurry*. I guess. I don't know!"

I thought back to when we were at her house earlier. *Had I seen something in the window after all?* Suddenly, my heart pounded. *What if she's been in distress this entire time? Lexi was right. We should have gone in—or at least scouted around more.* Then those thoughts flipped. We don't know she's at home; she could be anywhere.

"Bella, let me see her texts again."

I noticed the shorthand—'cll me asp' instead of being spelled out. But there was nothing that revealed her location.

"Did she leave voice messages?"

Bella scrolled. "Um, there's one … at six-thirty. That wasn't long ago!" She played it. There was little background noise and then we heard grunts, maybe a bang. "That's what she sounded like just now on the phone!"

Greg picked up his keys. We knew what needed to be done.

CHAPTER THIRTY

Ink black darkness infiltrated the entire neighborhood except for the glow of interior lights emanating from behind pulled curtains for a few homes. Cars sat in driveways and lined the street now; much different than it was earlier in the day. I pointed out the house at the same time Bella did. Shadow woofed.

"Park over there—not right in front." I pointed across the street and a couple of houses away.

"It doesn't look like anyone is there," he mumbled. "What exactly is our plan?"

Bella rummaged through her bag. "I have a key."

Both Greg and I whipped our heads around in amazement. "Why do you have a key?"

"She wanted me to feed her cat one day. Forgot to get it back to her."

We each got out and quietly shut our car doors. Shadow pulled, eager to get on with it.

"Relax, girl. You've got to be quiet." With that, she let out a bark.

"Shhhhh!" all of us scolded.

We crept across the street, hoping there weren't any nosey people looking out their windows.

"So are we using the key and walking on in then?" I asked.

"I'll knock first. But I don't see Bailey's car here."

"You know Bailey?"

"Met her only once. She has a red VW."

"That VW wasn't Sydney's?"

"No, she doesn't own a car. Bailey drives her around a lot … and lets her borrow it regularly too."

We approached the front door. Greg moved in toward the doorbell.

"Wait. Let's listen a second," I suggested.

Bella rolled her eyes. "For what?"

"To see if others are here…"

"I just told you, Bailey isn't here."

"What if the car is in the garage?"

"It's full of junk—no way to fit a car in."

Greg rang the doorbell. No sounds we could detect. He prompted to hurry, using his hands. "Okay, use the key…"

Bella fumbled around and finally got the key to work. As the door creaked open, she yelled out, "Sydney! Are you home?" She felt along the entry wall and flipped the light switch.

We stepped through one by one, with Bella leading the pack and Greg bringing up the rear. Shadow tried nosing around Bella, but I cinched her leash tight. The kitchen was the first room we came to on our right. It was a disaster—dishes piled high in the sink, every countertop and table piled with junk. We continued toward the living room straight ahead.

"Sydney!"

Shadow barked and pulled me toward a hallway just off the living room. "Shhhhh…"

Bella turned on a light in the hallway and followed us. "Her bedroom is the last one on the right."

I noticed the other three doors were closed. "Hello!" I yelled out as we crept along.

Shadow barked ferociously.

"What was that?" Greg called out.

Bella opened Sydney's bedroom door and her cat ran out. Shadow ignored the cat, but pulled hard to get inside the room. Then we heard a thud.

"Sydney?" I hollered.

Another thud.

"The bathroom!" Shadow dragged me to a door and pushed it open.

Sitting in the bathtub was the frightened girl. Duct tape across her mouth and wrapped around her wrists, which were laying in her lap. Her legs were crossed and large zip ties held her ankles, her phone sitting below her crossed legs.

Greg ran to her. "This is going to sting, but I'll be quick." He ripped the tape from her mouth before finishing his warning.

"Owww!" she yelled. "Hurry! They're coming back."

"Knife? Scissors?" I asked.

"Kitchen drawer."

I ran fast, rounding the corner and seeing the chaos.

How was I to find anything in this kitchen? Pulling out drawers as fast as I could, I plowed through looking for anything sharp. Glancing at the mayhem in the sink, I spotted a large knife. I grabbed it and took off again.

A light shone through the front room window. *Shit!*

We cut the ties off Sydney's ankles. "I saw what could have been headlights. Bailey might be home?"

Greg asked for the knife, and I handed it to him. "Bella, Libby, quick … find items to use as weapons. Sydney—you said *they* are coming back. Who? How many?"

"Bailey and her brothers. Three."

"We need to get out of here. Where's the back door?"

"Living room…"

Crap. We had to pass the front hallway to get there.

"Oh, oh, oh! There's a patio door off Bailey's room. I'll show you."

We all heard it. Keys in the door and voices from the outside.

"Hurry!" I said, running from Sydney's bedroom.

We scurried into Bailey's room, went in, and closed the door behind us. And I thought the kitchen was cluttered. There were boxes piled everywhere where furniture wasn't. Scrambling not to trip over boxes and piles of clothing, Sydney made it to the back door.

"Greg, help!" Bella hissed.

More boxes blocked access to the door. Greg went for the heavy boxes, spilling one over in the process. We began throwing items out of the way. I noticed much of what we handled were arts and crafts items. *This little thief!* I kept tossing stuff when I came across a pair of stylish combat boots. *Exactly as I'd seen previously—bet it was Bailey snooping around those booths.*

Then I lifted an opened box ... hundreds of posters poured as the bottom fell out. Distracted, I picked one up—*Tempe Arts & Crafts Festival posters?* That made no sense.

We all froze in place when we heard a man's voice boom from another room. "I don't remember leaving lights on earlier."

Another answered, "We didn't."

"Libby! C'mon!" Greg whispered, urging me through the door he'd opened. "Hurry!'

Shadow barked.

We bolted.

CHAPTER THIRTY-ONE

If I thought that the kitchen and Bailey's room were atrocious, the backyard was pure wreckage. And that was precisely what happened when we tried to run through it.

Greg went down. "Arrrgh!" he yelled, just as a gigantic dark figure overtook him. "Run!" he screamed to the rest of us.

My face felt every thistle scrape from the overgrown desert foliage as I fought my way through. Just when I saw the side gate destination, someone grabbed at my clothing, pulling me backward and slamming me into the ground. Or was it a bed of cactus? The electric impulses screamed throughout my body.

Shadow sounded ferocious. I peeked through my pain and saw her pulling on the leg of a large person.

I couldn't move. At least not until I felt my body being forcibly dragged away. Sharp objects slashed at my skin, my clothing no protection at all. I screamed out in agony, kicking with all my might. The man was powerful.

I heard punches landing and men grunting. Greg wailed as loud as he could, "Let her go!" before more punches cracked against someone's body.

Where were Sydney or Bella? I prayed they made it out in time. *Surely, the neighbors would hear the ruckus and call the police.*

Losing sense of time, but realizing I'd been dragged back inside the house, I heard a woman's voice. It wasn't Bailey; the voice sounded much older. Through swollen eyes, I tried desperately to see who my captors were. *Where was Shadow?*

The whole task was pointless, everything was blurry and distorted. My mind whirled—where had they taken Greg? The last I remembered, I knew he was fighting them off, but I no longer heard him or felt him nearby. I hoped Shadow had escaped with Bella, but the last glimpse I caught of her showed her clinging onto some guy's leg.

Dizziness took over every time I attempted to open my eyes. How much time had passed? The older woman's voice sounded again. Although not too far from me, I could hear them clearly.

"What the hell are we going to do with them now? You two are idiots! Always have been…"

"Mom, you said, 'catch them'…we did!"

"I didn't want them injured, you fools!"

"In fairness, they kind of did that to themselves. Have you seen Bailey's backyard?"

A younger voice scoffed. "Have you ever volunteered to help me out?"

"It's *your* house," he argued.

"Shut up!" the woman screeched. "All of you are imbeciles! I asked you for only a few little pranks to scare people from the joining the festival again and you idiots screwed *everything* up! Now look at the trouble we're in."

"Mom, in fairness…"

"You too, Bailey … shut up! If it weren't for your stupid roommate, we'd be in the clear. How stupid could she be!"

I kept deathly still listening to the revelations, and hoping Greg was in a place where he could hear too. Praying he was alive.

I startled when I heard a bark. Shadow was somewhere close!

"I told you to let that dog go!" one of the male voices shouted.

"I did. I kicked it and told him to get lost! Damn thing bit me!"

Oh, I will kill this guy. No one kicks my Shadow!

Hearing a scuffle, I wasn't sure who was involved. I tried again, lifting my eyelids. They were sealed shut. Tucking my bound arms and legs in as tightly as I could, I grimaced in pain. All I could do was pray. *Please no one touch me—and please let them leave me alone.* I pictured the goons fighting each other again.

The crack of a gunshot deafened me.

I cowered, terrified.

Screaming came from all directions. The pain my body endured, trying to curl up in a ball, was excruciating. Not understanding how long I held that position, I startled wildly when something wet touched the side of my face.

"Get away! Leave me alone!" I shouted, unable to see or move my arms.

I felt it again, along with a brief whine. That's when I noticed the only noise now was coming from me, screaming. And the whine…

"Shadow? Where are you, sweetie?"

She nuzzled in and licked me some more. I'd never been happier to be licked by a dog!

"Libby!" I heard a man's voice call out.

Frightened, I tucked back into the ball. Shadow pawed at me, then barked a couple times. I told her 'Shh'.

"Libby! It's the police—we're here to help!"

Shadow barked urgently. I felt footfalls and the sound of a door opening.

"There you are."

I cowered.

"It's okay. We got them. You will be okay." Then I heard him talk into his radio. "We're going to need another ambulance."

I turned to face the sound of his voice.

"Oh boy, you've been beat up good."

"Where's Greg?"

"He's okay. He's talking to my partner now. Then you'll both get transported to the hospital."

For the first time since we entered Bailey's home, I relaxed. Shadow never left my side until they loaded me into the ambulance.

CHAPTER THIRTY-TWO

By the next morning, everything looked much clearer. Literally. The swelling in my eyes had gone down some and I could see my mom walk into my hospital room.

"Whoa! You're a sight!" she laughed.

"That's what I hear," I groaned.

Not long after her, Greg and Bella walked in.

Bella gasped. "I'm so sorry, Libby."

"You didn't do this, Bella," I said, chuckling. "Ouch, no laughing yet, I guess." Grabbing my side, I gently felt along. Through my gown, it was like reading braille, the bumps were so swollen.

Greg lifted his shirt, showing us a hideous rash-like redness. "Yeah, they've removed many cactus needles from us both. You definitely got the worst of it, poor baby." He lovingly rubbed the top of my head, which was about the only part that didn't hurt.

He caught the look on my face when the police officer walked through the door. "Don't worry, I called Chris. Your attorney is on his way."

Relieved, I let the officer know I'd talk once my attorney arrived. He stepped outside the door and I got a few more minutes to visit with Mom and Bella before they had to leave.

When Chris walked in, I quickly related the few important pieces I needed him to know. Then he allowed the police in and they interviewed both Greg and me. While telling our version of the events that happened the night before, I told them my theories for each crime we'd been investigating. Thankfully, we had an officer who was willing to listen. The only problem was, I still didn't have all the answers. Thankfully, the police helped answer some of my questions as well.

"I don't understand the motive. Why would Bailey and her mother cause all this harm? Why us?"

The officer cleared his throat. "From what I've gathered so far, I don't think it was intentional." He saw me sit up taller, ready to argue. "Just hear me out. Don't get me wrong, they are in a lot of trouble—intentional or not. However, it sounds as though it started as harmless pranks meant to scare the vendors."

I remembered what the woman—who now I knew for sure was Heather Knox, Bailey's mother—was yelling at her family about last night. She said something similar.

"Did they confess to that?"

"Bailey did. Ms. Watson corroborated. Ms. Knox isn't speaking *yet*. I'm pretty sure once she figures out her whole family turned on her, she'll start talking."

"So, if I've got this right, Heather and Bailey are huge arts and crafts buffs. They attend the annual Tempe festival every year and were angry about the popularity that the Mesa festival had gained. They believed if they could keep vendors from attending, they alone could shut down the Mesa event."

"Yep, that's about right. They were also former Tempe workers who had been laid off some time ago. They've always blamed the Mesa festival as the reason, but I suspect that isn't the case."

I looked around at the condition Greg and I were in. "That's ridiculous. All this for *what*? What exactly did they gain here?"

"I'll never get over how many stupid criminals there are out there. There's never good justification for crime, but these pranks certainly gained them spots in jail." The officer sat, shaking his head in disbelief. "You may sue them for damages, too. Including for your medical bills."

My injuries would go away, and I'd be fine. I kept thinking about Pupcakes & More. These fools may have irreversibly harmed their reputation. I was sure they'd sue. But that got me thinking about the dogs.

"Have they admitted to poisoning dogs?"

"Again, Heather has admitted nothing. Bailey told us it was her mom's idea, only she and her brother actually carried out the crime."

I hung my head. *Stupid, stupid, stupid!* Poor dogs. Needlessly ill over these petty people. And their owners, out hundreds in veterinarian fees.

I felt completely drained of energy. Before leaving, the officer told us we could be called for more questioning, but he thought he had all he needed.

"I'm going to let you get some rest," Greg said, squeezing my hand and kissing the top of my head. "I've got to stop by work."

"They're making you work today?" After all we had been through, I was horrified to think he'd have to work.

"No. But, I've got some paperwork to complete. Since I've already been released from here, I figured I would keep myself occupied by getting that done now. Hopefully, they'll release you later today?"

"I sure hope so. Not really sure why I'm still here."

"Libby, you've taken some good hits. I think they want to make sure your noggin hasn't been affected." He laughed as he gently tapped my forehead before kissing it.

"I don't think there's anything they can do about my *noggin*," I teased. "Come back soon to take me home." My bottom lip protruded, pouting.

"Will do, love."

* * *

Later that morning, Bella came back to check on me.

"Feeling any better?" she softly asked.

Groaning, I opened my eyes. "I'm sooo sore."

"I'll bet. They did a number on you."

"Bella, have you talked to Sydney? Please tell me she had little involvement with that group."

She hung her head. "Yes. We have talked all morning, and I'm afraid she's gotten herself in too deep."

I couldn't reach my water cup with the straw in it. Bella grabbed it and held it for me while I sipped.

"Tell me everything." My dry, scratchy throat croaked out the words.

"So, Sydney knew Bailey from her school days. I guess Bailey was the cool kid and ran with some tougher juveniles. Sydney always tried to fit in, but never really did." She swallowed hard, sighed, and then continued. "Bailey is the definition of a bully, and apparently she's bullied Sydney all her life."

"That's surprising. When we first met Bailey, I was completely convinced she was a professional. Nothing about her screamed bully."

"She also probably would have been better off going into acting. She's a great actress!" Bella laughed. Then her face got serious. "Sydney's version of what happened goes like this…"

She explained that several years ago, Bailey's mother, Heather, worked for the City of Tempe Parks and Recreation Department, but the department let her go. She blamed one of her long-time colleagues for leaving and starting a similar position in the rival city, Mesa. It was her opinion that person took her knowledge of what Tempe does so well with their annual festival and copied it. Ever since, the Mesa arts and crafts festival has tripled its size and, according to Heather, also lured its vendors away. Without the revenue, they scaled back personnel in the Parks sector.

For the past few years, Heather toyed with Mesa vendors, trying to make them rethink the leadership so they wouldn't sign up the next time. When that didn't work, apparently, she elicited her family to ratchet up the pranks. Well, they certainly did that.

"What was Sydney's involvement, exactly?"

"Oh man, she feels sooo bad. She claims she never really knew what they were doing. But when Bailey learned you were looking into the dog illnesses, she completely freaked out. Sydney thinks that's when Bailey started pressuring her. Knowing that Sydney worked at Dharma Inspired, her brilliant idea was for Sydney to plant that note in your therapy room, making it appear the client was the culprit. So basically, to throw you off her trail."

"Well, Sydney shouldn't have got involved..." I stated, still angry she'd destroyed my trust in her.

"She realizes that now. I think she was trying to show Bailey she could be one of the cool kids, though."

"For God's sake, they're not in middle school any longer!" I shouted, then grimaced, grabbing my throat.

Bella handed me the cup again, and I took a nice, long swallow.

"For what it's worth, she said after learning exactly what Shelly and Yvette were dealing with at Pupcakes, she tried to get Bailey to stop. That only made things worse. Heather threatened her ... *and* her grandmother."

"What? Wait, what was their involvement at my mom's booth?"

Bella sighed and looked away. When she looked back, her eyes were wet. "I know Heather had a conversation with your mom. No one knows whether that led to Julia's fall. Apparently, Heather confronted Julia, thinking she was Ms. Watson. When Sydney learned about that, she told Bailey she was out. She couldn't participate in their pranks anymore."

"And that's probably when I saw Heather confronting Sydney at the festival, too. She could have told me then! I asked her about who she was talking to. Instead, she lied to me."

"She was frightened."

I closed my eyes, trying to absorb all the details. It stung knowing that our employee tried to blame an incriminating message on one of our clients. Good thing I never got hold of the man, or he wouldn't still be a client.

"Who stole the Stitches of Love products? What about the Zen Zone bath bombs? Please tell me it wasn't Sydney."

She let her head fall forward.

"You are kidding me! Why?"

"Bailey asked her to bag up both business's products and hide them … said it would be funny." Bella rolled her eyes. "Sydney admitted to watching Kathleen punch in our container's code at closing one day. She hid the Zen Zone products in our container."

"And, Sydney didn't think to speak up when I was almost arrested for that?" My blood was boiling and now I knew for certain that she would not be welcome back into our business. Hopefully, the little scamp would spend some time in jail with the others.

Bella had no defense. She appeared equally abhorred by each revelation Sydney had shared with her.

"Well, I think I've heard enough for one day. She's confessed all this to the police, right?"

Bella nodded her head.

"You are not seriously thinking of maintaining a friendship with her, are you?"

Embarrassed, she shook her head adamantly.

"Good. That girl needs to reevaluate her morals." I smiled at my friend and reached out my hand. She took it and I weakly squeezed. "Thank you for filling me in. My anger is solely directed at Sydney. You know that, right?"

She nodded and tears welled up in her eyes.

"What's wrong?" I asked.

"I can never pick good friends."

"Oh, honey … don't blame yourself."

"I really thought she was going to help me be brave enough to visit my mom. Guess that won't happen now."

"Hey, don't worry. And, you know I'm here for you, right?"

She smiled, wiped a tear from her cheek, and nodded.

The doctor walked in and Bella quickly turned away to clear the remaining tears.

"Great news, Libby. You're going home."

CHAPTER THIRTY-THREE

The following weekend, we met at the Irish pub for their Sunday roast. Everyone was there: John, Jessica, Yvette, Shelly, Rachel, Chris, Lexi, JJ, Margie, Greg, Mom, Shadow, and me. We occupied a festive, large outdoor patio and for the entire afternoon, the laughter was abundant.

Everyone praised Shadow for protecting Greg and me when those thugs caught up to us. She loved the attention, and I was also fairly sure she kept getting scraps of food from beneath the table. No one confessed to doing so, but that's where she took up residence for the evening.

At first, I was concerned Chris might feel out of place among this crowd, but I was happy he could join us. Then I remembered it was my friend JJ who introduced him to me initially. The two of them chatted away, catching up on everything law enforcement.

John and Jessica apologized again for ever thinking I could have been the one who stole their product from them.

"It really looked like you on that film," Jessica admitted.

I agreed and admitted to doing several double-takes myself. However, I had known all along that I was nowhere in the vicinity. Thankfully, Chris also believed in me and helped point out the holes in that theory. Of course, it was even more help when the culprits ultimately confessed.

Shelly turned to my mom, "Can I ask? How much money did people donate to Children's Hospital?"

"Oh! We did so well!" She looked down the table to find the journalist, Rachel. "Thank you so much for the story on the news. It made all the difference. We still have some donations coming in, thanks to Just Ducky and my friend Kathy, but so far, we've handed over *four hundred thousand dollars!* That was only the cash donation. We could also give hundreds of knitted blankets and toys to the children, too, thanks to all the knitting groups that participated."

Everyone cheered, clapping loudly, then lifting their glasses. "To Stitches of Love!" Shelly shouted over the revelry.

Once the crowd settled down again, Yvette stood up. "Rachel, we owe you so much! The follow up investigative story that aired this week—" she got choked up. "Well, let's just say that we will keep our doors open!"

The group went wild again, before the questions began to flow.

"Did you ever learn *how* those idiots tainted the Pupcakes treats?" Julia asked.

"Apparently, Heather saw me constantly popping mints in my mouth. She told her daughter; Bailey and her numbskull brother found one of my canisters laying around. They crushed them into a fine powder. They claim it was easy—on the first day, we had people lined up and it was only the two of us working. Bailey, being the smaller of the two, slipped in the back and dumped the powder into several of the opened bags we used for handing out samples."

There were gasps as we all pictured the dog treats being tainted.

"And that was enough to get the dogs sick?" JJ inquired.

Rachel nodded her head. "In my investigation, several veterinarians said it really doesn't take much. A lick of toothpaste, a mint, any product with fake sugar in it can make a dog ill. Now, some are more susceptible than others, but xylitol in any of its forms is poison to an animal."

I turned to Shelly and Yvette. "Have you reached out to the owners?"

"Oh yes," Yvette said, nodding. "They were awesome. We let them know how sick we were, knowing that their babies had been harmed. Thankfully, none of them died. We have offered each of the families a lifetime supply of Pupcakes & More organic food. And I think they trust now that our company had nothing to do with the problem at the festival. Thanks to Rachel!"

Shelly looked lovingly at her partner. My heart warmed knowing they'd patched things up and were in a better space. My eyes roved amongst the friends and family around the table. Mom's smile was infectious—she looked great and had no further issues since being released from the hospital. Margie had told us Ms. Watson was extremely embarrassed by her granddaughter's actions. They never blamed the sweet grandmother for her grandchild's poor decisions. Mom added how she suspected Ms. Watson was working overtime knitting to compensate.

Greg shared his news about buying the land near the Superstitions while all the shenanigans were going on. Mom was particularly excited about that news. Everyone was, really—comments were plentiful on upcoming activities each wanted to share with him, now that he'll be a fixture in the valley.

By the time we wrapped it up, we agreed on a monthly gathering. John and Jessica were going to pick the spot for our next one. We hugged, and I veered off inside for the restroom before we got in the car. On the way out, I remembered the suspicious person from the last time we came here. That was Bailey, I had guessed from those darned combat boots. She was the lurking one who we chased several times—always up to no good. Strange bunch, that family. I was perfectly happy to never see them again.

* * *

By the next morning when Shadow and I walked into the spa, the last person I expected to see was Sydney, sitting in one of our lobby chairs. Shadow barked at her and she startled.

"Libby…" she began.

I held my hand up. "No need. You're fired."

Lexi opened the door, cautiously stepping into the tension, and eyeing each of us. "What's going on here? What are you even doing here, Sydney?"

Her head dropped forward, looking defeated. "I know. I know. I'm fired. But, I owe you an explanation."

"Is there any explanation?" I asked her, holding on tighter to Shadow.

Lexi showed sympathy and asked her to follow us to the office. To me, she pointed to Shadow and said, "Maybe she can hang with one of the ladies for a few minutes? We don't need her taking a bite of Sydney." She winked at me.

Sydney's eyes grew enormous at that mention.

"Yep, I'll meet you back there." I chuckled. Shadow would never hurt a soul, but it was evident Sydney wasn't her favorite, and I was fine leaving the girl with that impression. In fact, I'd only picked up on that tension over the past few weeks—how many times *had* she growled at Sydney over the past couple of weeks? Wow! I've got to pay more attention to the signs.

After securing Shadow with Diane, I joined Sydney and Lexi in the office and closed the door. I couldn't help myself and launched in on interrogating the girl.

"We welcomed you into our workplace ... our little *family*. What possible justification do you have for your actions, Sydney?"

"Now Libby…" Lexi held up her hand. "Let's give her a chance to talk."

I plopped down in the chair. "Okay. Talk."

"Um, first, I …" she wiggled around in her chair. Choking up, she muttered, "I'm sorry. I truly am."

I crossed my arms in front of me and glared at the crying young woman. I'm not one easy to anger, but this young lady had pissed me off.

"You see, I honestly had no idea what Bailey was up to." Her eyes met my distrusting ones, and she held her palm toward me. "I swear!"

Lexi sighed. "From what we understand, you took

items from Libby's mother's booth and the Zen Zone booth. What exactly were you thinking was harmless about that?"

She caught her breath, full-on sobbing now. "Bailey was someone I always wanted as my best friend. She was so popular! I wanted to fit in, too. Yes, I should have known better when she started being super friendly with me. Now I know it was only because I knew a couple of the vendors—you two and Julia and Margie. I'm so stupid."

She continued from the beginning—how she and Bailey were mocking her grandmother's knitting group. How old-fashioned and stupid in the twenty-first century. Bailey dared her to take all their knitted goods and throw them out. To show that she was cool, too, she did.

"But, I couldn't possibly throw them in the trash. So, I stashed them away. First at home, but I was sure Bailey would find them and then I'd pay. So one night, I snuck them back to the festival when everyone was gone. I hid them around the corner by the candlemaker booth."

We learned the dares got more brazen, and although she had nothing to do with the Pupcakes poisonings, Bailey had convinced her to plant the note in a massage therapy room.

"She'd been following you, Libby—everywhere. Bailey knew you were investigating. Heather also knew that Lexi was calling around looking to talk to her."

"Yeah, about that—" Lexi interrupted. "They never worked for the City of Mesa. Why tour our spa to 'approve' us? I haven't understood the whole purpose of that."

She shrugged. "I think they were scoping out your facility, hoping to learn how best to scare you from the festival. Not fully sure what they planned there, but from that visit, Bailey knew the layout and she learned what my duties were. You know, cleaning the therapy rooms after each session. It could be when she came up with her scheme for me to plant the note?"

"And have me blame one of our clients…" I added. "Wait, how did Heather know about our calls to the City of Mesa, if she never worked there?"

"She knows people."

I stood up, towering over Sydney. "And what? You think all this is justification, and you should get your job back?"

Sydney quickly shook her head. "No! I know you don't want me here. I only wanted to come tell you how sorry I am. I couldn't have been more stupid. This was a great job, and I completely blew it." Her voice cracked, and tears fell again.

Lexi leaned forward across the desk. "Sydney, you're right. It was a very stupid thing to get involved with this friend of yours. I hoped you learned your lesson and I pray the law will be lenient for you this time around. We're not going to press charges—" she glanced at me, seeing if I'd protest to that. "But I'm sure others will. Particularly, Pupcakes & More and their victims. Hopefully, you can convince a judge you weren't part of that—even so, you know you are guilty by association regardless, right?"

The admonished girl nodded.

"This is your official notice—your employment with Dharma Inspired Day Spa has been terminated, as of today. We will walk you to your locker, where you'll clear out your belongings. We will mail you your final paycheck on payday. In addition, we accept your apology and wish you well. Anything else to add, Libby?" She turned around and picked up a piece of paper from the printer.

I considered the gravity of what those awful people got Sydney involved with. I'd hate to see her fall into poor decisions with equally bad, or worse, people. "You know you have a good friend in Bella. I'd apologize. Maybe something could be worked out with her? I don't know, she was pretty upset. My best advice is to worry less about popularity and more about always doing the right thing. You are old enough—you know what's right and what's wrong. Make good decisions, Sydney."

Lexi handed her the termination paperwork and had her sign. I opened the door, and we followed her to the employee lockers. She grabbed the few items and we walked her out the front door. With her head hung low, she slunk down the sidewalk and disappeared, I assumed to the nearby bus stop.

"That breaks my heart," I said, still peering out the glass windows.

"Me too. She was great at the front desk. I sure wished it had worked out differently."

The remainder of the day, I rested at home. My beat-up body was thankful for lounging on the sofa and cuddling up with my dog. The only time I made an effort all day was to eat the tacos Greg brought home at the end of his workday.

"How'd you do at work today?" I inquired. "Aren't you sore after our conflict with those goons?"

"Oh yeah. But, you took a much worse fall than I did. And those cactus—" he grimaced, opening a beer from the fridge. By the time he took a chair next to me, I saw that sparkle in his eye.

"What's going on?"

His smile was half-cocked and those eyes were bursting to say something. "How'd you know?"

"How'd I *not* know? That grin … you are up to something!" I laughed, then grabbed my side. Too soon.

"I have news to share. Might be too soon?"

"Nah. Just share … I'm fine."

"They asked me to join Search and Rescue in Alaska! That's the paperwork I had to handle yesterday."

"What! To move there?"

"No, nothing like that. At least, not at this point."

Although stunned, I was genuinely happy he wouldn't have to sit behind a desk long term.

"I have so many questions. First, when?" I wondered.

"I leave in three weeks. As soon as I'm done here."

My eyebrows arched. I grimaced; they also still hurt. "I don't understand. How do you know there's a rescue going on weeks from now?"

"Ah, yes. It's actually more training than participating in an actual rescue—although Clive says there are always searches and rescues going on somewhere in Alaska."

"Wow, that sounds cool. How long will you be gone?"

"At least one month—possibly more."

Happy to hear he wasn't moving to Alaska, but also sad to be apart for an entire month, the only thing that came out was, "Oh."

"But I was hoping maybe you'd come visit partway through…" he wiggled his eyebrows. "We could do some exceptional hiking, kayaking, all kinds of adventures, Ms. Madsen."

I perked up. I was always up for an adventure!

Author's Note

This was a fun story to write, mainly because of how much I personally love attending arts and crafts festivals. But once I got started, it seemed like a no-brainer—my sister-in-law is an artist and she spearheads a fantastic charity called Just Ducky. That's where I got my inspiration for Stitches of Love! Of course, I asked for permission before adding her to the story. Yes, Kathy Dewey and Just Ducky are the only elements in this story that are based on facts.

To give you a little background...

Kathy and Phil Dewey started Just Ducky in honor and remembrance of their son, Nicholas Dewey, who sadly died from cancer at the age of ten. Inspired by Nicholas, and to divert from the sadness while he was undergoing treatments, they focused on lifting the spirits of all the children and their families while at the hospital.

The gift card donation started because during Nicholas' treatment sometimes the gift card drawer was empty when he had to have a needle poke or other exceptionally difficult procedure. So donating gift cards became the goal; children can use a gift card online to purchase a movie or game, which helps to distract them from being at the hospital. Gift cards can also supply a meal or a treat while inpatient or at home. Toy donations are just fun, who can resist giving a child in treatment something special and fun.

Following his passing, they continue what Nicholas had started. Every year, in his birthday month of May, they hold a fundraiser and gift the children's hospital where he was treated with donations. Everything from electronics and toys for the kids for entertainment, to gift cards and items that can help the families. Most times, as did with Kathy, Phil, and their other child, Lucas, families have to uproot to a different city for the treatments. Some of these donations can help them supplement meals out or pick up necessities from stores.

The most fun legacy that the Deweys continue to carry on in Nicholas' name is bringing joy to others through his jovial spirit. During his treatment, he gave all his doctors and nurses duck keychains with a card that said, "Cancer is Yucky, but You're Just Ducky." (see image below)

They were a hit then and they continue to make people smile today, as the Deweys still collect and share their rubber duckies all the time. Whether traveling, or out and about in their own town, rubber ducks bring smiles to many unsuspecting faces. Pictures are shared widely on social media—you just never know when you'll find one of the Dewey's duckies.

I encourage you to follow their story at: https://

www.facebook.com/Cancerisyucky. My favorite month is May when I donate to this campaign. Kathy shares lovely memories of Nicholas and always captures his fun, lighthearted spirit, along with great family photos. Stay tuned as we get closer to May; I'll share more in my newsletter.

Thank you, Kathy, for allowing me to share a little bit about Nicholas and Just Ducky as part of this story!

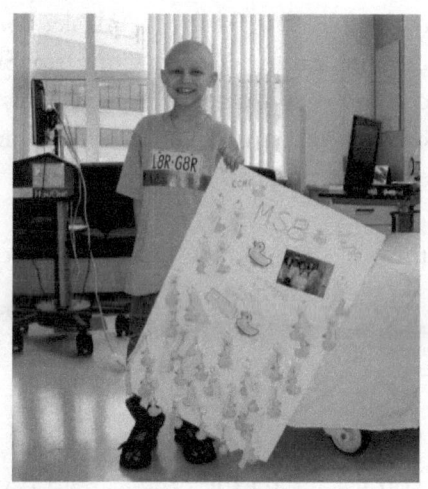

What's next for Libby and Shadow?

Libby, Greg, and Shadow are headed to Alaska, where Greg is getting Search and Rescue certified. He convinces Libby that Shadow should be evaluated at a world-renowned SAR Training Center. Libby isn't quite sure she wants to subject her beloved pet to the life of being a rescue dog, even though she'd probably be great at it. Meanwhile, there is a covert plan underway between Julia and Greg—he's asked Libby's mom for her blessing. The plan involves getting Libby to Alaska for a romantic getaway under the pretense of picking up Shadow after her evaluation. Between a tragic avalanche, missing musher pups, and activists blocking their path to solving anything, will Greg be able to pull off his proposal?

Don't miss Book 8 in this "impressively original and deftly crafted"* series!
*Midwest Book Review

* * *

Thank you for taking the time to read *Festive Shadows*. If you enjoyed it please tell your friends, and I would be so grateful if you would consider posting a review. Word of mouth is an author's best friend, and very much appreciated.
Thank you,
Jennifer Morgan

* * *

**Get another free book from Jennifer.
Scan the QR code to find out how!**

**Books in the Libby Madsen Cozy Mysteries
series:**

Shadows in the Forest

Spa Shadows

Shadowed Treasures

Shadow Retreats

Spooky Shadows

Shadow's Christmas Wish

Festive Shadows

The Christmas Fairy – a holiday novella

Let's connect!

Website: jenniferjmorgan.com

Email: jennifer@jenniferjmorgan.com

Facebook: https://www.facebook.com/profile.
php?id=100076154359528

Twitter: JenniferJMorga3

BookBub: https:bookbub.com/profile/433830544

Goodreads: 148099219-jennifer-morgan